W9-BVF-607

# Praise for

## DAWN OF THE ICE AGE

"*Lug* is a stone-cold fun read. The talented David Zeltser spins a clever prehistoric tale of friendship and adventure, with a charming trio battling some fearsome bullies and beasts as the Ice Age dawns. The humor is as sharp as the tigers' saber teeth."
**—Nathan Bransford, author of the Jacob Wonderbar series and *How to Write a Novel***

"Any kid who's not extinct should love Lug's rough-and-tumble romp through the world of dodo birds, jungle llamas, and cavemen."
**—Anne Nesbet, author of *A Box of Gargoyles* and *The Cabinet of Earths***

"David Zeltser's debut shows that courage takes many forms, and that the struggle to fit in while being true to yourself hasn't changed much in the past million years or so."
**—Barry Wolverton, author of *Neversink***

"David Zeltser has unthawed a glacier of a story that will melt your heart and leave you laughing out loud. Lug and his crazy cast of supporting characters deserve five caveman clubs for this hilarious saga of old traditions, dodo birds, and new beginnings."
**—Crystal Allen, author of *The Laura Line* and *How Lamar's Bad Prank Won a Bubba-Sized Trophy***

"Suspenseful and smartly humorous, this novel delights with its themes of brains over brawn and the power of friendship."
**—*ForeWord Reviews***

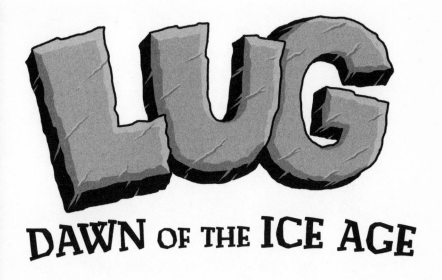

# LUG

## DAWN OF THE ICE AGE

by
**DAVID ZELTSER**

illustrations by
**JAN GERARDI**

EGMONT USA
New York

# EGMONT
*We bring stories to life*

First published by Egmont USA, 2014
443 Park Avenue South, Suite 806
New York, NY 10016

Text copyright © David Zeltser, 2014
Illustrations copyright © Jan Gerardi, 2014
All rights reserved

1 3 5 7 9 8 6 4 2

www.egmontusa.com
www.davidzeltser.com

Library of Congress Cataloging-in-Publication Data
Zeltser, David.
Lug and the dawn of the Ice Age / David Zeltser ; illustrated by Jan Gerardi.
pages cm
Summary: Lug is a cave boy who would rather paint than fight. When he
is banished from his clan, he and his two friends discover that the Ice
Age is coming, and must figure out how to save their people.
ISBN 978-1-60684-513-4 (hardcover) — ISBN 978-1-60684-514-1 (eBook)
[1. Prehistoric peoples—Fiction. 2. Glacial epoch—Fiction.]
I. Gerardi, Jan, illustrator. II. Title.
PZ7.Z3985Lu 2014
[Fic]—dc23
2014003144

Printed in the United States of America

All rights reserved. No part of this publication may be reproduced, stored in
a retrieval system, or transmitted, in any form or by any means, electronic,
mechanical, photocopying, or otherwise, without the prior permission of the
publisher and copyright owner.

*For my wife, Fiona, my daughter, Naomi,
and all the kids brave enough to speak up*

If you are looking at my cave paintings, I have succeeded. If not, we humans are probably extinct. You see, the world began to get colder—much colder. And my clan initially reacted by doing this:

That's right, a whole lot of NOTHING.

When that didn't work, we did something, but it might have been too late. If you, my clan's descendants, are still around, I hope this story will inspire you to pay attention to the big changes happening to your world. If you are extinct, sorry.

# ☞ 1 ☜

# BLOOD AND GUTS

**"OWWW," I MOANED,** gingerly feeling the plum-sized bump on my forehead. I opened my eyes and found myself sprawled and drooling on a cold limestone slab. From the golden tint of the light streaming in through the mouth of the cave, I judged that it was afternoon. *But where was I?*

Slowly turning my throbbing head, I glanced around and nearly fainted—there was blood pooling on the floor next to my face. Suddenly, a purple liver plopped into the red puddle with a *squish*. I breathed a sigh of relief.

My mother, Lugga, stood over me, gutting a big freshly killed dodo bird. Her long chiseled face, chestnut-brown hair, and banana-leaf top were speckled with bird blood and cave dust, and, as usual, she was up to her elbows in dodo guts. Next to her stood my father, Big Lug, a large, baby-faced, bald man with two chins and one tooth—and he did not look happy. He leaned on his trusty stone club, which was slightly bigger than me. From this close I could see the countless scars and blood-stains on his huge hands—the result of a lifetime of bashing things.

"You think that little bump *hurts*?" asked my

MY FAMILY

father as he casually reached into the dodo bird's chest and tossed a heart onto the glistening pile of guts next to me.

"Huh?" I said, rubbing my bump again and trying to remember how I'd gotten it. "What happened to me?"

"What happened to you?" My father's usually calm brown eyes were filled with worry. "What happened is that *you* wimped out!"

I had no idea what he was talking about, but I noticed that my mother's cheeks were wet with tears. I couldn't remember anything about the morning. Except for the mysterious bump on my head, everything in our family cave seemed normal. I decided it was best to pretend I knew what they were talking about. "You're right," I said, "I totally wimped out!"

"Don't be a Neanderthal," said Mom. "Do you have any idea how much trouble you're in?"

I swallowed and shook my head.

I heard a giggle behind me. My older sister, Windy, sat cross-legged at the back of the cave, plucking another freshly killed dodo. She had the round baby face of our father, minus a couple of chins. Lumpkin—our fat little cave cat—was lying on her lap, lazily batting at a floating dodo feather.

"What's so funny?" I grumbled.

"Nothing," said Windy. "Except how dumb you are. Does that bump on your head contain your entire brain?"

Leaning against the wall next to her was a small stone club I'd never seen before. "What's that?" I asked.

"That," said my father, "was supposed to be your caveman initiation gift."

"Oh," I said, trying to smile gratefully. "It's . . . it's . . . just what I've always wanted."

Windy laughed louder this time. "All you want," she said, "are some of those weird rocks that make colors."

"No I don't!" I lied.

My father frowned at me. I was a terrible liar.

"Dad," said Windy, "remember the time Lug got bashed in the head and ran home and made a little picture with his blood?"

My father's frown deepened.

That happened when I was five, but my sister

loved to remind us. A kid named Bonehead had bashed me with a rock and—to my everlasting regret—I had not bashed him back. But I had realized that I could use my blood to paint a colorful picture. It was awesome. I had bashed myself to get more blood, but then Mom made me stop. Later, when I was exploring a cave, I stumbled on a crumbly rock that had streaks of red in it. I crushed it into powder and discovered that, when mixed with spit, it made a beautiful bloody color that would stick to cave walls. Best day of my life!

"You better watch out," said my sister, "or you'll end up like Crazy Crag and—"

"That's enough!" snapped my father. "Windy, go and tell Boulder your brother's awake."

She stomped out.

My father and I sighed simultaneously. We had the exact same sigh. It was about the only thing we had in common.

"Why does Boulder need to know?" I asked, trying to keep my voice calm. Boulder the Bountiful was the Big Man of our clan, and I'd always had a feeling he didn't like me very much.

"Lug," he said, "Boulder is holding a Clan Council Circle about you right now."

"WHAT?" I stood up. "What do you mean?"

"I mean," he said, "Boulder wants to banish you."

# 2

## LITTLE SLUG

**THE MEMORIES CAME** back like a sudden volley of stones whacking me on the forehead. The trouble had begun when I'd leaned out of a dank hunting cave by the river that morning and peeked around at a herd of macrauchenia. The beasts had stood hoof-deep in the oozing mud of the riverbank, sucking up the brown water with their flexible little trunks and dumping it into their big toothy mouths. I had felt the cool wind gusting through the trees and shivered.

For months now, it had seemed to me that

our normally steamy jungle air had been slowly getting colder. The usually shiny green leaves on the gourd trees were a strange yellowish brown and now carpeted the forest floor. The beautiful red and violet orchids that normally grew in the sunny spots of the jungle had paled and shriveled. Even the gourd fruit—whose fuzzy pink shells my clan folk used to cover their private bits—were smaller this year, resulting in many uncomfortable glances and awkward silences. I had asked around and no one could remember seeing so many bare trees, not to mention bare bottoms. In my head a small warning voice had been growing louder and louder. "Lug," the voice kept saying, "this is *big*."

Yes, the events of the morning were all coming back to me. There had been seven other boys in the hunting cave with me. We were all about the same age, but I was the shortest and skinniest by far.

"You guys chilly at all?" I whispered to Chip and Rock, a tubby pair of twins.

"Shut . . ." Chip grunted, squinting his eyes like he was trying to remember something.

". . . up?" Rock volunteered.

The first twin gave a satisfied nod, confirming that *up* was indeed the word he was looking for. I looked around the cave at the other boys. None of these chunkers were shivering like me.

Rock pointed at the largest macrauchenia. "Good beast!" he grunted.

"Yah!" said Chip, ogling the animal. "Good for headstone!"

No one else in my clan seemed to care that it was getting colder. All they ever cared about was playing in the next big headstone game against the Boar Riders.

Headstone is a game where you bash the opposing players' heads with stones. In order to increase the risk of major injury, all players are also required to ride large animals while doing their bashing. My clan rode macrauchenia—fierce, striped jungle llamas with impressively long necks and short trunks—and so were known as the Macrauchenia Riders. Our neighboring rival clan—the Boar Riders—mounted huge razorback boars and got a big kick out of calling us Llama's Boys. Not to be outdone, my clan had dubbed the Boar Riders *Piggybacks*. Beyond shouting at each other every few years at the Big Game, the two clans never spoke. I had been taught that the Boar Riders were probably secret cannibals with no laws and fewer table manners, and that thrashing them in the Big Game was the most important thing a Macrauchenia Rider could do.

In our clan, a caveboy could only become a caveman by catching a wild macrauchenia, breaking it in, and riding it in the Big Game. If you failed at any step, you were considered unworthy, cast out into the jungle, and expected to politely die. In all the stories I'd heard, only one banished caveboy was said to have survived into cavemanhood. They called him Crazy Crag, and some people whispered that he was still out there roaming the forest. I'd never seen Crag myself but, if he was alive, I kind of envied him. I was pretty sure *he* didn't have to play headstone and could do whatever he wanted. Not that I wanted to be all alone in the jungle. I guess I just never felt like I belonged in my clan.

All the fathers had sat in the back of the hunting cave that morning and grunted excitedly. Tradition held that the boy who caught the biggest beast before the Big Game would someday become the clan's next Big Man.

*"Go, BONEHEAD!"* cheered Boulder the Bountiful, our current Big Man. Even in the dim dawn light, I could make out Boulder's hulking form in the rear of the cave. He had a blackbird's nest of a beard that hid his face in secret shadow—nearly everything but his eyes, which were a cold milky blue.

"Bonehead . . . head . . . ed," the cave walls echoed.

Bonehead glanced back at his father with a predatory grin. He was built like a slightly smaller version of Boulder except he was bristle-skulled, with small watery blue eyes and a thin-lipped mouth that had more gaps than teeth. But the most distinctive thing about Bonehead was the foot-long white bone that pierced his nose. He had once killed a baby jungle llama for it.

Unfortunately, Boulder's bellow did more than just encourage his son. It also startled several of the macrauchenia into glancing up.

BOULDER

"You first, Little Slug!" hissed Bonehead when he saw this.

I tried to ignore him, but his best friend, Bugeyes, chimed in. He was another specimen you wouldn't want to meet in a dark cave. Bugeyes was not as big (or dumb) as Bonehead, but he was twice as ugly, and with a surprisingly high-pitched voice for a kid his size.

"Lug's too small to be a slug," squeaked Bugeyes. "He's more like the flea I squashed in my armpit this morning!"

Bonehead laughed like a snorting pig.

The rest of the jungle llamas lifted their heads, craned their long necks, and peered at the cave suspiciously.

BONEHEAD

BUGEYES

"Biggest beast mine," Bonehead growled at me, suddenly serious again. "Got it, *flea*?"

I couldn't help staring at the repulsive little black whiskers sprouting above his lips and made a mental note to add those to my next painting of him.

"Fine with me," I whispered. I was much more focused on surviving the next hour than in becoming the tribe's next Big Man someday.

"Fine with me. Said *flea*!" jeered Bonehead, looking around to make sure everyone had heard this piece of poetic brilliance.

All of the other boys laughed nervously, not wanting to get on Bonehead's bad side. All except for a silent burly kid called Stony, who was gently cradling a bright orange tree frog with his thick banana-like fingers. Stony had wide-set hazel eyes and a wild tangle of dusty brown hair crowning his sloping forehead. Although Stony never spoke, he did have a very expressive unibrow. It wiggled on his low forehead like a giant fuzzy caterpillar as he flashed me a friendly, if slightly moronic, bucktoothed smile.

I turned away and forced myself to focus on the herd of macrauchenia. I hated being called small by Bonehead and Bugeyes but, as my mother liked to say, right now I had bigger stones to split. Despite their cute little flexible trunks, jungle llamas possess strong biting teeth and explosively powerful legs that can smash in your head like an overripe gourd fruit. I had spent many quiet mornings observing them and painting pictures of them on the walls of my secret art cave. I knew their strengths, but what were their weaknesses?

"Give me bigger stone." Bonehead's voice interrupted my thoughts.

I turned back and saw him trade with Bugeyes,

then tuck his new stone into his banana-leaf sash.

## The Macrauchenia Clan's Official
# STONE REGISTRATION SYSTEM

All privately owned stones
must be registered as one
of the following:

o Stone good for bashing
  someone because easy to hold
o Stone good for bashing
  someone because easy to hide
o Stone good for bashing
  someone in eye socket
o Sleeping slab
o Dining rock
o Boulder in front of cave (also
  known as door)
o Boulder not in front of cave
  (also known as obstacle)*

*You'll notice that "Stone good for art" is not

listed. Our Clan Council considers making art to be uncaveman-like behavior—a waste of time when you could be bashing perfectly good heads with perfectly good stones. That is why I kept my art cave a secret.

I tried to picture which way the jungle llamas would take off when all eight of us gave chase. Looking downriver I could make out the gray limestone cliffs that housed our village caves. Upriver I glimpsed the clearing that served as our clan's headstone practice field. Across the water, rising out of the jungle, loomed the great misty peak of Mount Bigbigbig. The base of its southern slope was not far from the opposite bank, but I had been taught that the mountain was sacred and should never be climbed. And I knew that beyond it was the territory of the Boar Riders. Of course, the other possibility was that the macrauchenia herd wouldn't run away at all, but simply charge the first boy to emerge from the cave.

"You first, Little Slug!" Bonehead commanded, elbowing me in the ribs.

I picked up a rock, fixed my gaze on a young doe—the smallest macrauchenia in the herd—and took a deep breath to calm my racing mind. Then Bonehead shoved me out of the cave.

"LUUUUUUUUG!" cheered a familiar voice from the back of the cave. I glanced back and was amazed to see my father smiling proudly at me. Then it dawned on me that he thought I'd charged out of the cave first. Of course, I hadn't charged out at all— I'd been thrown out. Still, my father was proud of me, and for a moment I was as happy as a dodo in springtime.

"YAAAAAAARGH!" roared Bonehead, shooting out of the cave just after me. He was followed by all the other boys—including Bugeyes, Chip and Rock, and the silent Stony bringing up the rear.

"YAAAAAAAAAAAAARGH!" roared our proud fathers in unison behind us. The macrauchenia chase was on.

\\||||/

I slowed down. My chosen doe was standing her ground, obviously unimpressed with me. When I was a short stone's throw from her, I stopped to see what all the other guys were up to. On my left, I saw Bugeyes brandishing a stone as he stared down a jungle llama that was desperately trying to look away. I could relate to that animal.

Behind Bugeyes, Chip and Rock had trapped two macrauchenia between themselves and the river. Then a sickening *thud* to my right revealed Bonehead grabbing hold of the largest beast and bashing it into submission with his rock. Only Stony and I did not have a llama, but Stony wasn't even trying. He was happily sitting on a rock, licking his frog.

"Think!" I said to myself, looking back at the doe. *"Think!"*

The doe charged.

*Bad*, I thought. *Very bad.* No chance of outrunning her, I desperately looked around once more. The llama followed my gaze and stopped a mere step away from me.

I knew I was supposed to bash it in the head with my rock, but I couldn't help admiring the animal up close. I observed the long graceful curve of her neck up to her strong jaw and found myself memorizing her subtly dappled fur pattern for my next painting. I peered into her big liquid-brown eyes, framed by lovely black eyelashes. After that, everything went black.

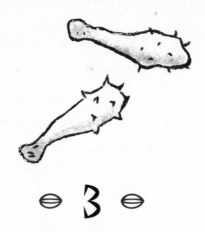

# ☰ 3 ☰

# A CAVEMAN COUNCIL

**"ONE HEAD BUTT** from that llama and you were out like a whacked dodo," muttered my father.

"Where are the rest of the guys now?"

"On the practice field, breaking in their beasts for the Big Game. Except for Stony—he's already at the Council Circle."

"They're going to banish him too?"

My father nodded and walked over to the back wall. He picked up the little club and brought it over. "Take it," he said huskily. He cleared his throat. "You're going to need it out there."

I found all my other thoughts swallowed up by a desperate wish that I hadn't disappointed him. Not today. Not ever.

"Don't cry!" I whispered to myself as I took the club. I knew that my father—like all cavemen—disapproved of crying. *At least if I'm banished,* I thought, *I'll never disappoint him again.*

Just then, my least favorite hairy figure darkened the cave entrance. Boulder the Bountiful lumbered in with his usual air of haughty menace. "Let's go," said Boulder to me, jerking his thumb behind him. "The Clan Council awaits."

"Boulder—please," my mother half whispered, "is there anything we can do?"

"Afraid not, Lugga," he said. "Clan rules."

My father turned away so that no one could see his face.

Even Windy looked worried as I walked past her out of the cave.

\\\\|/

A cold breeze nipped at me as I followed Boulder across the public clearing—a yard of packed dirt and scattered stones that served as a common area for the several dozen caves around it. Women and children peered at me from inside their dark entrances. Their looks suggested they might never see me again, which I found somewhat discouraging. Despite the clear blue sky, it was another strangely chilly afternoon. I turned away from the sun to look back at a series of jagged red cliffs to the east. There I could make out the long thin outcropping that marked my secret art cave—like a giant stone finger beckoning me.

I wished I could go there now and spend the rest of my life painting. Paintings didn't tell you what to do, or call you names, or make you feel small or worthless. And, unlike people, if a painting turned out to be unpleasant, I could always change it. Even better, if I didn't like a certain person, I could always paint their face to look like a Llama's b—

"This way!" snapped Boulder, yanking me out of my bright warm daydream into cold reality. He nudged me past the last home cave and around to the back of our village. We passed an unused drafty cavern and then the huge stable cave that housed our clan's captured jungle llamas. There was always a boulder in front of its entrance, but today there was also a caveman named Cliff guarding it.

"Any suspicious activity?" Boulder asked him.

Cliff shook his head. "Nothing, boss."

One of our clan's llamas had mysteriously disappeared from the stable cave a few days ago and everyone had blamed it on the Boar Riders. The odd thing was that they had never stolen a macrauchenia before, but no one seemed to care about that. With the Big Game coming, tensions were running especially high.

Boulder and I entered the jungle along one of the narrow llama trails that our clan used for moving through the thickest parts of the forest. We crunched along the strangely yellow leaves underfoot, the bare trees allowing the cold breeze to follow us into the jungle.

"No weapons in the Council Circle!" Boulder

suddenly barked, yanking my new club out of my hands. I thought I glimpsed a fleeting smirk beneath his bushy black beard, like the flash of a snake in the undergrowth.

We walked until we came to a clearing that used to be a beautiful orchid garden surrounded by thick green bushes. Now the flowers had all withered and only the yellowing bushes remained. A dozen cavemen sat on rocks around the circle, grumbling disapprovingly and looking very self-important. Stony sat on the ground in the center, petting his frog. I sat down next to the boy and he shot me a friendly arch of his unibrow.

Boulder remained standing and addressed the council in a booming voice. "You all know these two worthless weasels," he declared. "They have failed to catch even the smallest jungle llama for our clan. They are not worthy to be called cavemen." He took a long pause for effect. "Let us banish them!" he shouted.

Some of the men looked slightly uncomfortable, but a councilman named Frogface—who was Bugeyes's father—nodded vigorously. Then, one by one, each man nodded his head in formal approval of the Big Man's judgment.

Boulder was grinning slyly as he turned to Stony and me. "You, Stony, and *you*, Lug, are hereby banished from the great and honorable Macrauchenia Riders Clan!"

I stared numbly as Stony got up and wandered off along a llama trail as if taking a casual stroll. In moments, he had disappeared into the jungle.

"That's *it*?" I asked Boulder.

This time he risked an open smirk.

"But that's . . . not fair," I said.

The Big Man just shrugged.

"Look, I know you don't like me, but what about poor Stony? He can't even say anything to defend himself."

Boulder pointed a thick hairy finger toward the jungle. "You can both defend yourselves out there."

I thought I had one last hope. If I could somehow make myself useful to the council . . . maybe . . .

I turned to the other men. "It's been getting colder and colder out there!" I said.

There was a puzzled silence.

"What's your point?" Boulder demanded.

"Well . . . maybe we could all work together?" I said, my voice cracking with desperation. "You know . . . try to do something about the cold? I know you're all a bit more . . . um . . . well padded . . . than I am. But if it keeps getting colder, then we all might—"

"Little weakling is scared of a little cold!" Boulder sneered. "He is like the naked mole rat that eats the poo of a macrauchenia and lives in a hole in the ground."

"A true caveman doesn't care about *weather*," spat Frogface.

"Don't worry, Lug," said Boulder, "it'll get warmer again. But you will never be a Macrauchenia Rider."

I saw that there was no hope. "Can I at least

have my club back?" I asked. "It's a gift from my father."

The Big Man looked around as if he didn't know what I was talking about. "What club?"

I could feel the tears coming on when something just behind Boulder caught my eye. I cocked my head and peered at what looked like the end of a bone sticking out of the bushes. It quivered slightly.

"So," I said, looking back at Boulder, "not catching a jungle llama gets me kicked out, huh?"

The Big Man's eyes narrowed suspiciously. *"Yeah?"*

I pointed dramatically at the quivering bone. "Well, everyone knows that spying on a Council Circle is strictly forbidden!"

Boulder turned, his back hair bristling. He grabbed the bone and yanked it hard—dragging a yowling Bonehead out of the bushes. He might have pulled the bone loose from his son's nose and cracked the boy's skull with it if the foliage hadn't rustled again. Everyone watched as a sheepish Bugeyes stepped out after Bonehead.

I cleared my throat. "So, are you going to banish your own son too?" I asked, pointing at Bonehead.

Now I had him. Everyone knew that Boulder was grooming Bonehead to be the next Big Man. I was as good as off the hook.

Boulder's milky blue eyes darted around the circle. A thick vein pulsed in his forehead. And then a nasty little grin crossed his lips. "Bonehead and Bugeyes," he barked, "you are banished too!"

# 4

# INTO THE JUNGLE

**I WAS TOO** stunned to speak.

"B-b-but," stammered Bonehead, "but me next Big Man!"

I didn't stick around for that family meeting. I knew that as soon as Bonehead and Bugeyes were officially banished, they would seek vengeance by hunting me down.

"Stony!" I shouted, racing along the narrow llama trail that led to the river. "Stony, we've got to hide!"

I soon caught up to him and explained what

had happened after he'd left. Stony ambled over to a banana tree and lay down underneath it. Then he plopped his pet tree frog on his belly and started to play with the critter.

"For stone's sake!" I said. "This is serious!"

Stony glanced up meaningfully at the banana tree's huge withering leaves.

"Oh," I said, suddenly understanding. I plucked off the biggest leaf and used it to cover his bare belly.

He giggled with ticklish glee.

"Quiet!" I whispered, lying down next to him and putting another leaf over his chest and head.

He squealed with laughter.

"Enjoy your last laugh," I said, covering my own body with a single leaf, "because if they hear us, we're *dead*."

Stony's next giggle was cut short.

"What did your dad say?" Bugeyes asked as he came into earshot.

"If us kill Little Slug," Bonehead replied, "us back in clan. Look, he even give me new club."

"Your dad's nice!"

"Yah," said Bonehead, getting closer. "When me Big Man, no more Mister Nice Big Man."

"Look!" Bugeyes screeched.

"What?" grunted Bonehead.

I heard a dry twig crack nearby and caught a whiff of stinky feet.

"On the ground," said Bugeyes. "Banana leaves."

*Well, that didn't take very long,* I thought. I peeked up from the ground and saw Bonehead holding the new club my father had given me. I almost jumped up and grabbed it, but I didn't want him playing whack-a-dodo with my head.

Instead of going for the leaves covering Stony and me, Bonehead yanked a banana from the tree. Bugeyes did the same. Then each stuffed an entire unpeeled fruit into his mouth and began to chew like pigs.

"Li'l dry," said Bonehead, spitting out half the banana as he spoke. "Better with water."

Bugeyes chewed thoughtfully and nodded. I sighed in relief as they walked off in the direction of the river.

Suddenly, I heard a loud rustle beside me.

I poked a hole in my banana leaf and peeked out. Stony was frantically looking around, jostling the leaves on top of him. Bonehead and Bugeyes had stopped and turned around.

*"Stony!"* I whispered. "What's the matter with you?"

He pointed up and gasped. His little orange tree frog was climbing the trunk of the banana tree.

"Keep still!" I whispered. "We can't do anything until they're gone."

The frog was stalking a fat green praying

mantis perched on the trunk. The frog was so fixated on the mantis that he seemed unaware of Bonehead and Bugeyes.

"Hey!" squeaked Bugeyes, his eyes bulging even more than usual. "It's Froggy!"

The frog froze, staring back with equally protuberant eyes—perhaps wondering if Bugeyes was some sort of giant relative. Froggy gulped nervously.

Bonehead turned to Bugeyes. "What?" he asked. "Want eat frog too?"

"No . . . it's orange!" said Bugeyes. "It looks like Stony's Froggy."

Bonehead made a sudden grab for the creature. Froggy leapt onto Bugeyes's shoulder. Bonehead swatted at him but whacked Bugeyes hard instead.

"That's my face!" shrieked Bugeyes.

"Ribbit!" went Froggy, leaping onto Bonehead's nose bone.

This time it was Bugeyes who swung hard.

"OWWWWWWW!" screamed Bonehead, rubbing his throbbing nose as the little croaker leapt into the air. Then he punched Bugeyes in the forehead.

Froggy landed squarely on Stony's upturned palm, which had suddenly popped out between the banana leaves on the ground.

Bonehead and Bugeyes looked down, mouths agape. Even the aloof praying mantis cocked his head admiringly.

"Stony!" I shouted, springing up and taking off. "Follow me!"

He dashed after me, frog in hand.

"Little Slug slow!" screamed Bonehead, waving my club just behind us.

"And Stony's stupid!" cackled Bugeyes.

I jumped in first. My feet squelched in the mud as my lungs gasped at the shock of chilly water. I had not thought the river would feel *this* cold. But as soon as I was up to my neck, Stony lifted me up onto his shoulders. Froggy glided speedily ahead of us with twitchy little kicks. Bonehead and Bugeyes—still shouting—splashed in after us.

It was a long hard swim but, finally, we

emerged soaked and shivering onto the opposite bank.

"Follow me no matter what!" I said to Stony, and sprinted ahead. I had an idea.

We couldn't hear our pursuers now, but I knew that wouldn't last long. Sure enough, after a few moments, I heard Bugeyes's screechy voice. "Hey!" he shrieked. "They're going up Mount Bigbigbig!"

I glanced back and saw a wide-eyed Bonehead stop dead in his tracks. "No one go up Mount Bigbigbig!" gasped Bonehead, shaking the club in the air. "Mount Bigbigbig sacred!"

Stony caught up and shot me a nervous sidelong glance.

"Just up a little bit," I gasped. "Trust me."

We didn't go up very long before I shifted course so that we ran parallel to the jungle below. The vegetation was thinner up here, which made it a little easier. Soon we saw the great Headstone Field below us, a huge natural clearing dotted with countless rock-slide stones ideal for head smashing. There was a long-standing agreement between both clans to avoid the field except on the day of the Big Game. So I decided the jungle just above it would be the perfect place for us to rest.

I lay down on the ground, thinking we'd get right back up again. We must have been truly exhausted because my last memory of the day was Stony and Froggy cuddling. I wondered how the tiny animal had gotten so attached to this huge boy. But watching the two of them, I realized there was something about Stony's natural gentleness that might attract all kinds of creatures. Even though he wasn't much of a talker, I decided that I liked Stony.

\\\\\\/

I got up at dawn and stretched my stone-cold limbs. We headed back toward the river for a drink, and I noticed that the foliage on this side of the water was denser and darker. There were fewer gourd trees and more multi-trunked banyans. Tangles of strangler vines crisscrossed in every direction, creating excellent hiding spots for creepy crawlies of all kinds. Oddly, several banyan trees seemed to have been trampled. What beast could have done that kind of damage, I wondered. Even the biggest razorback boars didn't get *that* big. Was it the same thing that had taken the missing llama from my clan's stable cave? My thoughts were interrupted by the sudden absence of footsteps behind me.

"Stony?" I said, glancing back.

Stony's unibrow leapt up under his bangs and writhed like a worm in the shadow of a bird. I followed his gaze toward a thick stand of banyan trees. From the early morning shadows emerged a half dozen fierce-looking men, each astride a razorback boar.

We stood frozen, not daring even to breathe.

The biggest man I had ever seen broke the silence. "Bring Llama's Boys to me," he growled.

I peed my gourd.

# ☙ 5 ☙

# PIGGYBACK

**"WE'VE GOT LLAMA'S** Boys!" bellowed the Boar Riders' Big Man, effortlessly lifting Stony and me above his head.

As we entered their village, a few small children ran alongside the mounted procession, shouting, "Llama's Boys! Llama's Boys! Boss Hog's got Llama's Boys!"

I was stunned to see that the Boar Rider village looked very similar to my own clan's. I'd been told that these people lived in filthy wet holes unfit for naked mole rats, but instead I saw many cozy-looking caves surrounding a public clearing of nicely packed dirt. Even their rocks looked clean.

Smack-dab in the center of the village, glinting in the late afternoon sun, stood the Shiny Stone.

The Shiny Stone was a slightly shiny stone. It was also the trophy for the Big Game. The winning clan received the privilege of displaying it in their village until the next Big Game. Boar Riders of all ages began to sing spiritedly as we passed by it:

> *When Big Game comes*
> *and time to fight,*
> *we kick your bums*
> *and show our might!*
> *Grind Llama's Boys*
> *to llama's bones,*
> *and always KEEEEEP . . .*
> *great Shiny Stone!*

Peeking above the stone was a pair of wide green eyes underneath a tangle of red curls. As far as I could tell, this girl was the only one who wasn't singing.

||||/

Boss Hog led us down a boar trail behind their village caves. I thought about the stories of Boar Rider cannibals and noticed Stony sucking in his stomach to try to look skinnier. Then I cleared my throat and addressed the Big Man. "Excuse me, O Huge One?"

He ignored me.

"O . . . *Gigantic* One?" I ventured, my voice cracking a little. "Have you noticed how bony I am?"

Nothing.

"O Humongous One! My friend here licks frogs. You really wouldn't want to eat him."

"Eat?" grunted Boss Hog. He stepped aside, and I was astounded to see a circle of seated men in a small clearing down the trail. "We're going to the Clan Council."

"Wow!" I blurted out as we approached. "You guys do that too?"

*"Too?"* growled the nearest councilman, giving me a nasty snort. He had greasy red hair and small piggish green eyes. "I know you Macrauchenia Riders live like animals. You don't have laws or councils."

"How do you know that, Snortimer?" asked a nearby councilman.

The red-haired Snortimer eyed the guy for a moment. Then he whacked him in the head with a rock.

Boss Hog dumped us in the center of the circle and looked at us questioningly. "Is Snortimer right about you?" he asked.

"No," I said, "we have a council! We were tried and banished today." I cringed as soon as I said it.

There was a long silence as a dozen suspicious faces studied us. Stony took the opportunity to smile idiotically at them.

Snortimer's green piggish eyes bore into mine. "He lies!" he suddenly announced, jumping up and pointing at me. "He's a little spy."

I glared at him. I would have been okay with *spy*, but *little spy* hurt.

"You here to steal the Shiny Stone?" he demanded.

I shook my head. "Of course not."

"Then why are you spying on us before the Big Game?"

"I don't care about the Big Game!" I snapped.

A great raucous laughter went up around the circle. The Big Man guffawed uncontrollably, his jowls and belly jiggling in unison. Even Snortimer smiled.

"And I don't want to be a part of any big stupid clan," I blurted out. "I just want to be left alone."

Boss Hog turned to the council, wiping away the tears of laughter. "What do you think I should do with these silly spies?" he asked.

"Give them up," said Snortimer. "To Big Mumma." There was no mirth in his voice now.

But what scared me even more was the look on Boss Hog's face. He was the biggest, toughest man I had ever seen, and even he looked appalled. He began to waddle toward us, but Snortimer got to him first.

"If you back down, boss, you'll look weak,"

I heard Snortimer whisper to him. "And no one wants a weak Big Man, right?"

Boss Hog nodded sheepishly and stepped back.

\*\*\*\*\*

The Boar Rider councilmen led Stony and me back toward their village's central clearing, where a buzzing crowd was starting to gather. Not far from the Shiny Stone, the girl with the big green eyes watched us, now fidgeting anxiously with a curl of red hair. Snortimer stood with us in the clearing, facing a cave entrance blocked by a massive granite boulder and two huge men guarding it.

"Want to see what we keep in there?" he shouted for all to hear.

We shook our heads.

"Then admit you're spies!"

"But we're—"

"Say it!"

"What?"

"You're spies!"

"You're spies," I said.

There were titters from the crowd.

Snortimer's face flushed. "Oinker! New-porker!" he barked at the guards. "Release Big Mumma!"

The nervous laughter suddenly turned into shocked gasps.

Snortimer grinned, then nodded to Oinker and Newporker. The men leaned their shoulders into the big round boulder and grunted. The boulder began to roll, inch by inch, gradually revealing the entrance to a dark cavern behind it. There was a hushed silence.

Little by little, a great hairy boar snout emerged from the darkness. It was longer than my arm and had cavernous moist pink nostrils the width of Stony's fists. The snout took a cautious, almost delicate, sniff of the air. First in one direction, then another, gingerly sampling what the breeze had to offer. Seeming to catch a whiff of something interesting, the great snout turned toward us.

I shuddered. Stony shuddered. Even Froggy, on Stony's shoulder, shuddered. We had never seen a snout of this magnitude, and we didn't want to meet its owner.

"Big Mumma's hungry," said Snortimer, backing away from us toward the crowd. "Big Mumma loves new treats."

Suddenly, a stupendous sow—all muscle and bristle—charged out of the cave.

"Run, Stony!" I screamed, and promptly followed my own advice.

Glancing back, I saw that the low-browed boy had just stood there, holding Froggy protectively to his chest.

When the monstrous sow had nearly reached him, Stony closed his eyes and gave the frog a lick. This must have surprised Big Mumma as much as everyone else, because she came to a sudden

halt—her wide wet snout a hairbreadth from Stony's face. The crowd murmured nervously as she proceeded to sniff the boy and frog. It seemed that only Stony's tight grip prevented the accidental inhalation of his beloved. Then the sow's mouth opened and a huge pink tongue emerged. The crowd gasped. She gave Stony and Froggy a lick.

The boy beamed. The frog looked astonished. Big Mumma's monstrous expression melted into simple delight. She batted her eyelashes at Froggy. Stony reached out and scratched the sow under her snout.

I noticed that Snortimer's eyes were slits of fury. Everyone began to chatter animatedly.

Then Snortimer held up a hand for silence. "Boar Riders!" he boomed. "Boar Riders—I know the spies' secret plan!"

The crowd grunted questioningly.

"Llama's Boys," he said, pointing helpfully at us, "plan to bring frogs to the Big Game!"

The crowd grunted louder, though still questioningly.

"To make our beasts all *nice-nice*, of course!"

he snarled, pointing at Big Mumma, who was now nuzzling Froggy.

Most of the Boar Riders appeared impressed with Snortimer's theory—some utterly dazzled. Everyone looked to see what Boss Hog thought, but he looked clueless.

"We'll crush them, right, Dad?" shouted an eager voice from the throng. It belonged to a huge scowling boy who looked a lot like Boss Hog and sported a necklace made of pig vertebrae around his thick neck.

"Not now, Baconbits," grunted Boss Hog.

Baconbits turned his impressive scowl onto Stony and me and thunked a massive fist into the palm of his hand.

"Almost makes me miss Bonehead," I whispered.

Stony's unibrow perked up at this, and his eyes scanned the nearby trees.

"Bonehead and Bugeyes are the least of our problems now," I murmured.

# ⊜ 6 ⊜

# ECHO

**ONCE THE CROWD** had dispersed, Snortimer unceremoniously stuffed us inside a tiny dark cave and blocked off the entrance with a boulder. The space was so tiny and dark that it was less a cave and more a vertical tomb. There wasn't enough room to do anything but stand there and involuntarily cuddle. Even Froggy—normally an enthusiastic cuddler—croaked about the appalling lack of personal space.

Stony remained silent, but I could hear both our stomachs rumbling with hunger.

"Any ideas?" I finally whispered.

"Ehhh?" grunted Stony.

*"Ideas?"* I said more loudly.

"Ideas . . . deas," came the echo.

"Wait a minute," I said, struggling to reach up into the darkness above me. "I can't feel a ceiling."

"Ceiling . . . eiling."

Stony tried jumping up.

"Ow!" I said, removing his palm from my face.

He lifted me and pushed me up along the wall and onto his shoulders. I could feel the slimy circular sidewalls around me, but still no ceiling. We were like two mice stuck at the bottom of a snake hole.

By the time I managed to wriggle back down into the tight space between the wall and Stony's belly, he was snoring. I just stood there, impressed by his animal-like ability to snooze standing up. I tried closing my eyes, but it felt strange to sleep in a cave that wasn't my family's. Normally, I'd be able to hear my father's even louder snoring now. I found myself wondering what my parents were doing. This somehow made me feel a little better and much sadder at the same time. I realized that the dull empty ache in the pit of my stomach was not only hunger but also dread that I might never see my family again.

I awoke suddenly—slumped and cramped—in total darkness.

"Croak, croak" went Froggy, next to my ear.

"Croak, croak" came back the echo.

"Croak, ribbit" went Froggy.

"Croak, ribbit" came back the echo.

"Croak, ribbit, ribbit, croak" went Froggy.

"Ribbit, croak, croak, ribbit" came back the echo.

"Stony," I whispered, "did you hear that?"

His response was a snore in my other ear.

I nudged him. *"Wake up."*

He grunted groggily.

"I think there's something in here!" I whispered. "Something froglike, but bigger."

"Don't you have any manners?" a girl's voice asked primly from above.

Startled, I elbowed Stony in the belly, causing him to grunt louder as he awoke.

"I guess not," said the voice. "Well, then, I suppose there will be no need to rescue you."

There was a brief silence as Stony and I contemplated this in the dark. I cleared my throat. "Excuse me," I said, "who are you?"

"Echo."

"Very funny," I muttered.

"That *is* my name. And it's not stupid."

"Who said it was?"

"I can tell you thought it was from your tone."

She was right—I had thought that.

"Excuse me, Echo," I said, "but did you say something about rescuing us?"

"*Yes?*" she said, as if waiting for something more.

"Well, feel free!"

"Don't you have something you'd like to say first?"

"Ummmm . . . no," I said. *"Ow!"* I could feel

Stony's elbow in my chest and his expectant stare in the dark. "Fine," I muttered, surprised at Stony's reaction. "I'm sorry I made fun of your name."

"And?" said the voice.

"And? . . . I'm sorry I called you froglike?"

There was a long silence.

"All right," she said, "I'll rescue you. But mainly because your frog sounds nice."

A few moments later, I heard scrabbling sounds and a shower of pebbles hitting a hard surface nearby. This turned out to be Stony's head. Then I felt something tickle my neck. I reached around and grabbed . . . a vine!

"Go ahead and pull yourself up," said Echo.

I started doing just that, but she cleared her throat and added: "In order of politeness, please."

"Politeness?"

"That means your friends first. I found you to be least polite."

I sighed and felt around in the dark for Stony's hands. "You're going to need both of these," I said, sticking Froggy in his mouth.

After a bit of huffing and puffing, the

low-browed boy began to shinny up the vine using the circular wall around him for footing. Soon I heard the girl say, "And where is your frog, sir?"

I tried not to laugh, but when I heard the girl give an astonished squeal, I couldn't stop myself. That's when I felt the vine jerk out of my hands.

"Are you enjoying yourself?" she called down.

"Um . . . no, no, not at all."

There was another silence.

"*Sorry,*" I said. "Can I come up now?"

The reply came in the form of the vine whacking me on the head.

"Ow."

The first thing I saw as I squeezed up and out of the cave tube were silhouettes of the girl and Stony, standing in a large upper chamber. My eyes adjusted to the light and I saw that she was the red-haired girl who had stood behind the Shiny Stone—the only Boar Rider who hadn't taunted us.

"Thanks," I said, dropping the vine, which was cleverly tied to a stalagmite. "I'm Lug."

"Echo," she repeated, her bright green eyes daring me to challenge her.

"Crooooooak!" came a call from somewhere within the girl's tangle of red curls. She reached up and petted Froggy, who was peeking out of her hair. He looked very self-satisfied.

I rubbed my arms in the morning air. We had climbed out of the cave's upper chamber onto a high outcropping above the Boar Riders' village. Looking out over the jungle canopy, I saw that the banyan trees had also suffered from the cooling weather over the past few months. They hadn't lost all their leaves like the gourd trees, but their top branches were bare, pointing like gnarled accusing fingers at the milky sky. In the distance, Mount Bigbigbig rose like a great rocky island out of a green and brown sea of jungle, looking eerie as ever. My sister had once told me that the restless ghosts of banished boys wandered its slope, looking for any living clan folk who strayed too close. I normally ignored everything my sister said, but somehow that had stuck with me.

The Boar Riders' public clearing lay below— empty except for the Shiny Stone glimmering slightly in the dawn light. A cacophony of snoring and gassy sounds came from the caves around us.

"We'd better go," whispered Echo, "before someone wakes up and sees us."

We followed her down the other side of the outcropping and into the forest, in the direction of the mountain. The canopy was full of buzzing and birdsong, and by the time we came to a burbling creek, I had relaxed a little. I took a drink from the stream and thought about ways I might paint flowing water. But Stony's wary expression reminded me that Bonehead and Bugeyes were probably still skulking around, hunting us. Bonehead's words to Bugeyes came back to me, as clear as the burbling creek: *If us kill Little Slug, us back in clan.*

We followed the creek downstream, clambering over the slippery tree roots along the water's edge and keeping an eye out for water snakes. Eventually, we came to what seemed like an extremely wide boar trail. Echo led us up the trail, away from the creek, and I told her the story of how Stony and I had been banished. Several times I stopped talking, thinking I'd heard something moving in the foliage, but I decided it was just the wind rustling the leaves. Finally, we reached a towering pile of boulders not far from the base of the mountain. Echo climbed up the stones and slowly scanned the forest below, trying to make sure that no one had followed us.

When we reached the top, she pointed down the other side of the boulder pile toward a large, dark cavern entrance. "Okay," she said. "Follow me."

"I'm not going in there," I said.

She turned her head slowly toward me.

"I—I just mean I've had enough caves for one day."

She sighed and started climbing down the boulder pile, with Stony just behind her.

I muttered darkly to myself and followed.

At the mouth of the cavern, Stony began to sniff the air.

"Ready?" said Echo.

"Ready for what?" I asked.

She took a step into the cave and called out, "Woolly?"

"Woolly . . . oolly," came back the echo.

"Come out!"

"Come out . . . out."

"I'll be right back," she said, and disappeared into the cave. "Woolly can be a little shy."

"I think this girl's a little woolly in the head!" I whispered to Stony.

He shook his head and sniffed the air vigorously.

"We need to stop wasting time," I insisted, "and figure out a way back into our clan. If we catch a couple of big llamas, I think they'd let us back in. We could see our families. The Big Game is in two days, and they're not going to turn down any player with a good animal."

Stony's unibrow began to squirm like a caught eel.

"Yeah," I said, "it's going to be hard, but—"

Stony shook his head frantically and pointed

ahead. I stumbled backward. The massive creature lumbering out of the cave was unlike anything I'd ever seen. The beast had a trunk like a macrauchenia, but this was no little dangly thing. It reached all the way to the ground and swung ponderously, like another great limb. On either side of the trunk was a sharp white tusk. And above those were two enormous brown eyes that peered down suspiciously at us from beneath a mop of shaggy hair. The animal had a body like a boulder, a broad sloping back, and a high-domed head with wide flapping ears. He was covered from head to toe in long woolly shags of reddish-brown hair that hung down around his four tree trunk–like legs.

"Don't make any sudden moves," warned Echo, stepping out of the cave. "He doesn't trust strangers."

Stony and I stood perfectly still. "What is he?" I whispered, watching the long hairy trunk sniff inches away from my face. "Some kind of monster macrauchenia?"

"He's a woolly mammoth," said Echo. "A little one."

# ⊖ 7 ⊖

# THE BEAST

**"A *LITTLE* ONE?"** I croaked.

"Yeah," said Echo. "He's very young."

"Okay . . . but . . . how come we've never seen one before?"

"Because he's not from around here. I stumbled onto him when I was exploring the jungle. My clan doesn't know about him, and all I know so far is that something terrible happened and he got separated from his herd."

"Because of the cold?"

Echo looked confused. "What?"

"Never mind," I said. "How did you learn all this?"

"You mean you haven't figured it out yet?"

"Figured what out?"

"I can talk to animals," she said.

I studied her face, trying to determine if she was completely crazy or, as my mother liked to say, just had a few stones loose.

"So can you," she added. "I think."

I glanced sidelong at Stony, but he was just standing there, stroking Froggy contentedly.

"I think anyone could do it if they paid enough attention," the girl continued. "Of course, only some animals will talk back."

"Look, we really appreciate you rescuing us and everything," I said, backing away, "but maybe we should just say good-bye here."

"Good-bye? I brought you here so that we could take Woolly back to your clan."

"*What?* What would he do there?"

She gave me a long, knowing look. "Oh, come on!" she finally said. "*Everyone* knows that you Macrauchenia Riders live in the same caves as your llamas. My clan says it's primitive and dirty, but I think it's much kinder to the animals. Honestly, I don't care if you have no laws or councils. As long you treat your animals better than my clan does, Woolly will be happier there."

"Are you kidding me?" I said. "My clan is just like yours."

Echo looked at Woolly, appalled.

"If we brought this beast to my village," I continued, "they'd . . . stone him!"

She burst into tears.

"Okay, okay," I said, "Stony and I will try to help you find a safe place for Woolly, okay?"

She looked from me to Stony, and he added his most reassuring bucktoothed grin. Then he handed her a soft leaf from a nearby shrub and gestured toward her face. She took it and blew her nose.

"But first," I continued, "we need to find a macrauchenia for the Big Game. It's the only way our clan will even *consider* letting us back in."

"Wait," said Echo, brightening, "you just asked me if Woolly was some kind of monster macrauchenia."

"Yeah?"

"So let's bring him back to your clan and say that's what he is! They'd treat him well then, wouldn't they?"

I gave the young mammoth an appraising look. He did look like he could take out about five boars at once. "Maybe," I said. "*If* he could help win the Big Game, they'd treat him very well. They might even let Stony and me back in the clan."

"Perfect!" she said. "It's settled, then."

I shook my head. "You're forgetting one absolutely impossible thing. To play in the Big Game, I would actually have to *ride* that monster."

Echo smiled, grabbed a handful of Woolly's hair as if it were a vine, and clambered up his side. "Not impossible," she said, settling in just behind the young mammoth's head. "And you could say I'm his trainer. That way I'd get to live with him too."

"*You?* With *my* clan?"

"Well, *my* clan isn't going to take me back now that I've helped their prisoners escape, are they?" she said. Then she whispered something in Woolly's ear.

He nodded.

I suddenly remembered how Echo had been croaking back and forth with Froggy when I'd first woken up in the tiny dark cave. Maybe she really could talk to animals. I'd heard tales of my great-great-great-grandparents doing that sort of thing, but they had been monkeys themselves. I had thought I was living in a more advanced era. "Echo," I said, "do you really think I could ride him?"

She looked from Woolly to me. "You're going to have to talk to him about that."

"Talk to him?"

"Yeah," she said. "I don't know if you've ever

tried to have a conversation with a frog or bird or cat, but talking with a mammoth can be slightly trickier. For one thing, if he doesn't like you, he can stomp you flat."

Stony and I watched her shinny down one of Woolly's legs like it was a mossy tree trunk, and I wondered just when those huge round feet had last trampled someone.

"Not that he would stomp you flat," she added.

"Of course not," I muttered.

"Maybe just a little stomp."

Stony grinned.

"Very funny," I said.

"We should have some breakfast," Echo declared. "No one likes training on an empty stomach."

"Fine," I said. "I'll go find us a dodo."

"Not for me," she replied. "I don't eat animals."

I stared, thinking I must have misheard her.

"It's wrong!" she said.

"Wrong? Dodos are delicious."

"*Why* is everyone around here *obsessed* with eating dodo birds? You can't throw a rock without hitting a dead dodo, or someone eating a dead dodo. It's primitive!"

"Um . . . they're delicious."

"And that's all you care about?"

"Well," I admitted, "I have sometimes worried that if we eat too many of them, there won't be any left."

Now it was Echo who looked confused. "What do you mean?"

"You know," I said, "like they will go extinct."

She half laughed, half snorted. "Dodos will never go extinct! *Extinct?* Now, *that's* ridiculous!"

〢〢〢〢

After taking a drink from the creek, I set off down a sun-dappled boar trail to see what I could forage for us. I followed it toward the shadiest section of the forest at the base of Mount Bigbigbig. Here, in the cold shadow of the mountain, I noticed that even the hardy strangler vines had lost all their blue flowers and had very few leaves left. All the bare branches and vines around me made me feel like I was inside a giant skeleton with no meat on its bones. I wished the rest of my clan could see this part of the forest—maybe it would convince them that something big was happening. Then a tiny burst of color caught my eye. I stooped low in the shadow of a dead tree and saw a single red-and-yellow orchid. Since the arrival of the cold, nearly all the orchids had shriveled and wilted. And yet, somehow, this single blossom had managed to survive in the shadiest part of the jungle. I thought about picking it and painting it, but I didn't want to risk destroying what might be the last of its kind.

I got up and walked around the rotting trunk. This was the perfect root-cracked soil for finding edible mushrooms.

I gasped. On the other side of the dead tree, leaning against a half-rotted root, was the severed head of a boar.

I gazed at its blank, unseeing, but perfectly intact eyes, oddly fixed in my direction. The rest of the boar was nowhere to be seen, though judging by the head, it must have been enormous. Even more strangely, the head had a large puncture wound through the skull and another identical one through the snout. I knew of no creature with teeth big enough to make holes like that. *Unless*, I thought, *these wounds were made by tusks.*

"The beast is near!" whispered a scratchy voice behind me.

# ⊜ 8 ⊜

# EVERYTHING CHANGES

**I JUMPED SEVERAL** feet in the air and swung around. A pair of sprightly blue eyes peeped at me out of a wrinkly, gray-whiskered face. The man was lean, almost heronlike, and his head was as bald and leathery as a snake egg. It was as if all of his hair had crawled off his scalp and formed under his nose into whiskers as gray and bushy as squirrel tails. I took a step backward. I'd never seen him before but I knew in my gut who he must be.

"Crazy Crag," I said, trying to sound matter-of-fact.

He seemed to wince momentarily at this, but it was so fleeting I couldn't tell for sure.

"I'm Lug," I said.

"Dinky Lug!" he chortled.

I stared at him.

"*Runty* Lug?" he asked, stroking his mustache. "Or . . . Stunted Lug?"

"My name—"

"Wait, wait, one more guess!" he said, rubbing a pair of strangely gray-smudged hands together. "Is it Little Slug?"

"I don't like to be called that."

"Really?"

I nodded, taking the hint. "I guess you prefer to be called just *Crag*, then?"

"Actually, Crazy Crag has a lot more *oomph* to it," he said. "I've also heard them call me Cracked Crag, and I have a very special place in my heart for Cuckoo Crag."

I gawked at him.

"Confusion is good," he said. "It's a sign that you might actually be paying attention."

I inched backward, even more confused.

"Most people just don't pay attention," he continued, his blue eyes twinkling. "They don't notice little changes here and there." He wiggled his fingers toward a stand of bare gourd trees. "And then—*poof!*—everything suddenly changes and they discover they've been fools all their lives."

I eyed the bare trees, stripped by the cold. "What do you mean *everything* changes?"

He grandly waved a hand toward Mount Big-bigbig and the sky. "There's always something bigger coming around the mountain."

I felt my eyes pulled back to the two bloody holes in the boar's head.

"Don't worry, my piddly pebble!" he chortled. "The beast won't get you. Not if you stick with Crazy Crag."

"There's . . . a beast?"

"Many!" said Crag, pointing behind me toward a rustling sound.

I whipped around, fists clenched. It was just a little spotted squirrel on a branch. It chittered and scampered off.

Crag giggled.

"That," I said, trying to regain my composure, "was not funny."

"Come to my cave," he said, pointing toward the mountain. "I control the storm light. Beasts don't like storm light."

I inched farther back. "I just want to know who killed this boar."

"What a *boring* question!" he said, yawning.

"O-kay," I said, "um, what do you want?"

"A better question. What do *you* want?"

I glanced at the boar's head again. "An answer."

"I'm afraid all I have is questions," he said, stretching luxuriantly. "Off to my cave now. The question is, do you want to see the storm light that makes the beasts fear you? Especially in the dark."

"I'd . . . love to," I said, taking another step back, "but . . ."

"Late for lunch?"

"I really gotta go!" I said, taking off.

When I glanced back, Crag was smiling and wiggling good-bye with his gray-smudged fingers. "I'll see you *sooon*," he sang. "When there's no *mooon* . . ."

For a moment, I wondered how his fingers had gotten that dark, rich gray color. It was a hue I had always wanted for my paintings, but I had never been able to find a rock that could produce it.

He turned and strolled up the slope, his song fading out as he disappeared into the foliage. "When there's a *stooorm* . . . one must stay *waaarm* . . ."

I had an unsettling feeling that I'd be seeing him sooner than I'd like.

\\\|||/

I ran back empty-handed and found Echo by the burbling stream. She was watching the young mammoth use his long, muscular trunk to suck up the water and dump it into his mouth. It was very similar to how a macrauchenia drank, except a jungle llama couldn't strangle another animal with its tiny trunk. I studied his two wet, sharp tusks, gleaming bright white in the late morning sun. They looked just the right size to have made the wounds in the boar's head.

"Echo," I whispered, "what does he eat?"

The mammoth's big ears seemed to perk up at this.

I took her aside and told her about finding the severed head.

"Woolly wouldn't touch a boar," she said. "He's a plant eater like me."

"How do you know? Maybe he eats other things when you're not around."

"Because his poo isn't all stinky like a meat eater's. Believe me," she said, "we plant eaters know each other."

I was considering whether to tell her about Crag, when Stony returned. He carried so many bananas and gourds and berries that he looked like a walking fruit basket. Froggy sat on his shoulder, squinting sinisterly at the cloud of cheeky little fruit flies that hovered around them. The frog flicked out a long pink tongue and swallowed the nearest one with a smug little gulp.

After we'd all eaten, Echo suddenly stood up. "Lug," she said, "Stony, Froggy, and I are going to leave you and Woolly together for a while. If you're going to ride him in the Big Game, you guys need to get to know each other."

I shot the young mammoth a suspicious look. "I guess so," I muttered.

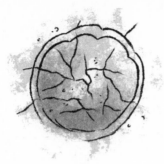

# 9

# A Short Chat with a Mammoth

**ALONE NOW, WOOLLY** and I eyed each other, each waiting for the other to make the first move.

"Hello," I finally grumbled.

Woolly got up and lumbered off.

# ⊜ 10 ⊜

# CAVE ART

**WHEN ECHO AND** Stony returned they found me alone, finger painting on the wall outside Woolly's cave. I had found a chunk of red ocher rock, smashed some of it into powder, and added some spit to make it into red dye. They watched as I painted the head of the smallest figure in a scene of four people—two larger and two smaller— sitting around a dining rock.

"Your family?" asked Echo.

I kept my eyes on my work.

"Where's Woolly?" she asked.

I shrugged. "He hates me," I finally said. "He'll never let me ride him."

"He just doesn't trust you yet. He'll warm up."

"The Big Game is in two days!"

"Maybe if you trusted him more?"

"Why should I?"

"Because you need him."

"I don't need anyone," I said.

"You don't *think* you need anyone! That's your problem."

I glared at her.

She glared right back at me.

"How," I finally said, "do you know that?"

"Lug," she said, "you just *told* me you don't need anyone."

"I just meant . . . I . . . wish I didn't. I wish I could just go and . . ." I glanced toward the distant cliffs that held my secret art cave. "Never mind."

She gave me a puzzled look.

Stony grunted and gestured toward the boulder pile. We all turned to look, and through an opening between two boulders, we saw a big brown eye watching us.

"Let's go," whispered Echo.

"Why?"

"Just trust me," she said, gesturing for Stony to come along too.

He followed, and I came trudging after.

"Woolly needs some time alone," she explained as we walked down the boar trail. "Besides, I want you to show me that boar's head you found."

\|\|\|\|\|

I led them along the trail until we reached the shadow of Mount Bigbigbig. After a little searching in the dim light, I found the dead tree near the solitary orchid.

"For stone's sake!" I said, scanning the ground. "It was right here, I swear."

We scoured the area but there was no trace of the boar's head.

Echo and Stony exchanged skeptical glances. "I bet Crazy Crag took it," I blurted out.

Stony's eyes suddenly got very wide.

"Crazy Crag?" said Echo. "Come on, that's just an old Llama's Boys legend."

"No," I said. "My clan banished him when he was a boy, and he's still alive."

"How do you know?"

"Uh . . . u-um," I stammered. "I didn't want to alarm you guys, but . . . I ran into him when I found the boar's head."

Stony's unibrow shot up.

Echo looked at me like I had more than a few stones loose.

*"What?"* I said.

Before she could reply, we heard the wood-splintering sounds of something massive running through distant foliage. It was followed by the faint *thud* of a smaller animal hitting the ground with a muffled squeal. A deathly silence descended. It was as if no bird or insect dared breathe, much less chirp or buzz.

"Something big is out there!" whispered Echo.

"I noticed!" I whispered back.

We stayed in place for a long time until the chirping and buzzing returned. When we finally got back we found Woolly resting on his side in a shady spot by the stream.

I eyed him suspiciously.

 ||||//

How was I supposed to ride a giant beast that I didn't trust? And if I didn't ride him, how would I ever see my family again? And if I did ride him, how was I supposed to avoid dying? These were the merry thoughts bouncing around my head as we bedded down in Woolly's cave that night. The dark reddish walls and the stalactites studding its ceiling made me feel like I was in the cavernous mouth of some great stone-toothed monster. There was old bat guano on the floor but, eerily, no bats—as if the cave had become too creepy even for them. Stony, Froggy, and I slept toward the back, while Echo curled up next to Woolly, closer to the entrance.

The wind woke me in the middle of the night. I had goose bumps on my arms and legs. I glanced over at Echo. Her face seemed dangerously close to those sharp tusks, which gleamed ominously even in the dim moonlight.

"Echo," I whispered. *"Echo?"*

No response.

I crawled over and poked her shoulder.

"Sleeping," she mumbled.

I waited for more, but she kept her eyes closed. "Echo . . . do you feel like . . . like it's been getting really cold lately?" I asked.

"I said sleeping," she muttered a bit more clearly.

I listened to the gusting wind and shivered. "It's not right."

"Oh, for crying out loud." She pushed up onto an elbow. "Why do you think I'm sleeping next to a woolly mammoth? Did you need to wake me up for this?"

"Aren't you worried that it might keep getting colder and colder, until—"

"Until what?" she snapped.

"I don't know," I said, "but I have a feeling it won't be good."

Echo closed her eyes. "I know it's been getting

a little colder, but I don't think it's a big deal. A lot of people in my village have been saying we could use a little cooler weather."

"This doesn't feel like weather. It feels like a major change. It's never gotten this cold before."

"I'm sure it'll warm up again."

"What if it doesn't?"

"It's the middle of the night, Lug."

"Finally," I muttered, "something we agree on."

"If you're so cold, ask Woolly if you can sleep next to him. It's nice and warm under his fur."

"And what if he rolls over and crushes us? Did you ever think of that? He's not some fuzzy little cave cat, you know!"

"Good night, Lug." She snuggled back into the woolly mammoth and closed her eyes.

I rolled over, grumbling to myself.

〢〣〢

I awoke to a scraping sound. I rubbed my stiff limbs in the faint dawn light and saw that Echo,

Stony, and Froggy were still asleep. It took me a moment to remember that there had been a woolly mammoth in this cave last night. "Where'd you go, you oversize cave kitty?" I murmured.

I crept over to the entrance and peeked out. What I saw made me pinch myself.

Woolly stood outside the cave, holding the last remains of my lump of red ocher with the tip of his trunk. Near my painting of my family there was now a crude drawing of two mammoths—a larger one and a smaller one—huddled close. I stared for a long time.

"You . . . and your mother?" I finally asked, trying to hide my amazement.

Woolly turned and looked at me. He gave a slight nod.

I nodded back at him. "And . . . what about your father?"

This time the young mammoth looked down. It was just a small gesture but there was something heartbreaking about it from such a big, tough-looking beast. I reached out and touched his side, petting his thick reddish-brown fur. It was much softer than I had expected.

After a while, he looked up at my painting again.

"I miss my parents too," I said. "More than I can say."

Woolly reached out and gently touched my back with his trunk.

# ⊜ 11 ⊜

# A SMALL CHANGE
# IN PLANS

**"WOOOOHOOOOOO!"** I whooped, riding Woolly past the cave as Echo and Stony set up another target gourd.

The young mammoth grabbed a large rock with the tip of his trunk and whipped it around.

I winced as it missed the fruit and smashed loudly against the wall near the cave entrance.

"Woolly," I said, "try a smaller rock."

He ambled over to another stone and rumbled something in his own language.

I glanced at Echo. It was all gibberish to me.

"Don't look at me," she said. "Pay attention to him."

I listened to Woolly repeat his rumbling. The last part sounded like a question. Something like *"MMMUOUOUAJAAAM?"* Suddenly, a bit of the meaning became clear to me. "Good?" he was asking as he held up the rock. "Good?"

"Yes!" I replied. "That rock is a good size!"

He picked it up, examined it briefly, then hurled it at the target. The gourd exploded into a hundred pieces.

"Nice throw!" I said.

"I know," he replied. (Well, it sounded like *"CHOUAUO AUAAARRP,"* but I was pretty sure it meant "I know.")

I whooped and shot Echo a smile. She had been right after all—I could communicate with an animal if I paid enough attention.

"Okay, Woolly!" I said after he had smashed yet another gourd fruit. "Now . . . turn."

He circled around with surprising agility and charged back in the opposite direction, kicking up a dust cloud worthy of a rock slide.

When Echo had finished sneezing, she beamed at us. "You guys should be ready for the Big Game in no time!" she said.

卌

After smashing every gourd fruit in sight that morning, we were worn out and starving. Echo went to forage and returned with a bunch of pale, hideous, rootlike things she called vegetables.

"Are they practice targets?" I asked.

She rolled her eyes and took a big crunchy bite out of something that looked like it should have definitely stayed in the ground.

"Now, *that's* wrong," I said.

"This is from someone who eats things that move and poop and sing."

It was only after she ate three of these monstrosities and did not die that I finally tried a vegetable. I chewed very slowly, trying my best not to gag.

"Well?" she asked.

"Delicious!" I said, spitting it out behind a bush as soon as she turned away.

I got up to rinse my mouth in the stream.

"*Hamela?*" said a small, unfamiliar voice from atop the boulder pile.

We all looked up. A little red-haired boy no more than six years old squeezed out from between two boulders and started clambering down toward us.

"Oh, no . . . no . . . no," muttered Echo, clearly mortified.

"Hamela!" shouted the boy, smiling and waving to her as he scrambled down the rocks.

I looked at her. "*Hamela?*" I said, trying to keep a straight face.

She glanced at Stony, who was also smirking a little. Even Woolly looked amused. She groaned. "Yes," she muttered, "that's the name I was given."

"You—"

"However," she cut me off, "since I do not eat ham or any other animal parts, I would prefer that you continue to call me—"

"*HAMELA!*" shouted the boy, running over

and hugging her. He had the same bright green eyes as hers, but his were twinkling in delight. "You are in soooo much trouble!" he said.

"Everyone," she muttered, "this is my little brother, Hamhock."

"What's THAT?" asked Hamhock, pointing at Woolly.

Echo sighed and led her brother away from everyone, into the cavern.

As the siblings caught up on everything that had happened, Stony and I stood outside the entrance and eavesdropped.

"It was easy," I heard Hammock say. "I followed you out here one time before. So I guessed you might be here again. When are you coming home?"

"After the Big Game tomorrow," said Echo. "As soon as Woolly is accepted by Lug's clan, you and I can hang out and play skipstone together, okay?"

"I guess," said Hamhock, sounding unsure. "Can I go pet that big critter now?"

He darted out of the cave toward Woolly, and Echo trudged over to us, shaking her head miserably. "We'll have to take him with us."

"I think those vegetable things are messing with your head," I said.

"Lug, if Hamhock blabs everything to my clan, they'll find us and kill Woolly! Not to mention you guys."

"But we're already taking *you* to my village," I said. "Taking another Boar Rider kid is not part of the plan."

"Younger brothers have a way of changing people's plans."

"Hey, I'm a younger brother."

"So you know all about it," she said, marching over to Hamhock and helping him up onto Woolly's back.

"Wow!" I said. "I didn't think it was possible to be bossier than my sister."

"Hamhock," she said, holding him in midair. "Do you want to play skipstone with me tomorrow?"

"Yeah!" he said.

"Then when we get to Lug's village, I don't want you to say a word. Not a word. Is that clear?"

The little boy nodded.

The really strange thing was that I had started missing my sister too. And since this plan was the only one I had for seeing my family again, I sighed and climbed up Woolly's side, settling in just behind his massive shaggy head.

Stony quickly followed, sitting behind Echo, with Froggy on his shoulder.

"Okay, Woolly," I said, pointing in the direction of my clan's village, "let's go."

\||||/

Treetops shot by, the ground rumbled—it was like riding a superlow, superfast thundercloud.

I knew there were two main obstacles between us and my village—the mountain and the river. We could simply ride *around* the base of Mount Bigbigbig, but the cold water would have to be crossed.

In what seemed like no time at all, we could smell the heavy, moist scent of the river in the air. Banyans were giving way to more and more gourd trees. I knew my village was in the jungle on the other side.

"AAAAAAH!" we screamed in unison as Woolly plunged into the water.

But the river turned out to be more fun on a mammoth. Woolly gamboled through the water like a piglet through a puddle.

"Hold on tight!" Echo warned as the mammoth lumbered out onto the bank. He shook himself, spraying cold water in every direction.

I looked upriver and saw some very familiar forms riding jungle llamas on my clan's muddy practice field. I took a deep breath. "This is it," I said.

Woolly made a complicated grumbling sound.

"Yes," I said. "We really need to impress them today. Even though the Big Game isn't until tomorrow."

He nodded once.

"All right, then," I said, giving him a pat on the head. "Let's show them how we charge!"

〰〰〰

My clansmen halted their macrauchenias and stared wide-eyed as the biggest beast they'd ever seen charged onto their practice field.

"*Hey!*" I said, spotting Bonehead and Bugeyes. "How did those maggots manage to worm their way back into the clan?"

"Good question," said Echo. "You don't look dead to me!"

"Huh?" squeaked Bugeyes, halting his llama. "Little Slug?"

"No way!" grunted Bonehead.

"Change of plans, Woolly," I said, pointing at Bugeyes. "That one!"

The mammoth reached out with his trunk and

snatched the screaming bully off his macrauchenia.

"Into that one," I said, pointing at Bonehead.

Woolly tossed one brute at the other. Bugeyes knocked Bonehead off his mount, and they both landed in an oozing mud puddle with a satisfying *thwap.*

Most of the mounted Macrauchenia Riders approached slowly, but one bald man trotted ahead of the others, chins jiggling. "Lug!" he cried.

I wanted more than anything to climb down and hug my father, but I knew he wouldn't approve. "Hi, Dad," I said.

"What are you riding there?" he boomed with obvious pride. "It's huge!"

I scanned the other men's faces. Most were looking at Woolly with a mix of interest and fear. I took a deep breath. If our plan was going to work, the next thing I said had better go over. "This," I said with as much authority as I could muster, "is the world's most monstrous macrauchenia!"

"But that's not—" Hamhock said, and suddenly stopped talking upon catching sight of his sister's glare.

Boulder, who rode the largest jungle llama in the clan, trotted forward and made a slow circle around Woolly, eyeing him suspiciously. "Why does it have tusks like a boar?" he demanded.

"Because," piped up Echo, "it's not *exactly* a macrauchenia."

Boulder looked at her out of the corner of his eye, like she was a buzzing mosquito he'd like to swat.

"You see, O Bountiful One," she continued, "my clan bred our biggest boar with the most massive macrauchenia we could find. Thus creating a *boarauchenia*—the greatest headstone beast of all time!"

"Ooooooooooooh!" went the other players, crowding forward. (Their animals looked more skeptical.)

"And who are *you*?" Boulder snarled.

"I," she said, "am this boarauchenia's t—"

"Target!" I interjected.

Echo looked at me in surprise. The plan had been to say that she was Woolly's trainer.

"Target?" asked Boulder, clearly intrigued by the concept.

"That's right!" I said. "Those lawless Boar Rider cannibals were using their own kids to give this monster some headstone target practice. I saved these two pathetic children and tamed the boarauchenia!"

Echo shot me a look that said *I will bash your head in later,* but she had to content herself with muttering darkly under her breath.

"And now," I cried, "this beast is going to win us the Big Game and bring home the Shiny Stone!"

The crowd of players started chattering like monkeys.

My father rode over to Boulder and bowed his head. He looked exhausted. I could tell by the dark circles under his eyes that he hadn't slept much since I'd been gone. "Big Man," he said, "now that Lug has caught a huge beast, maybe he can return to the clan?"

"And Stony too?" chimed in Stony's father, Stoner.

Stroking his beard, Boulder studied the young mammoth coldly. "*If* the boarauchenia helps us win," he announced, "they're back in."

"YAAAAAAAAAA!" cheered Big Lug, Stoner, and several other cavemen.

I shot a twitch of a smile at Echo and Stony. The plan was working!

Boulder took advantage of the men's distraction to lean in close enough for me to smell his putrid breath. "And if we lose," he whispered, making a slow throat-cutting gesture, "you lose."

Out of the corner of my eye, I noticed Bonehead and Bugeyes slowly sitting up in the puddle and staring at me. Their faces were dark with mud, but their eyes were alight with the steady cold glow of pure hatred.

# ⊜ 12 ⊜

# BIG GAME

**THE NEXT DAY** I awoke at dawn to find my parents and sister still asleep. It was fantastic to be home—the night had seemed almost warm in the cave with my family. I listened contentedly to my father's rumbling snores and stared at the scratches on my mother's forehead. Windy had told me that our parents had secretly ventured into the jungle at night to try to find me.

I climbed off my sleeping slab and crept over to the old chipped dining rock in the center of the dim chamber. It was still heaped with dodo parts from the welcome dinner my mother had made last night. Lumpkin was sleeping on the rock as usual. The fat little cave cat half opened one drowsy yellow eye and then promptly shut it. I quietly gathered up some leftovers and slipped out into the early-morning light.

I found Echo and Hamhock asleep next to Woolly in the normally unused drafty cavern behind the village.

"Big day, people," I said. "I brought you dodo parts for breakfast."

"You're the dodo," Echo muttered, eyes still closed. "I'm a plant eater, remember?"

Unlike his bossy sister, young Hamhock took some dodo bits.

I gave him an encouraging smile. "You ready for the Big Game?"

"Yeah," he said, chewing thoughtfully, "we're going to bash you Llama's Boys today."

"Hamhock!" snapped Echo, sitting up and glaring at him. "Remember what I told you? We want Lug's clan to win so that they'll like Woolly and keep him!"

"And keep me alive," I muttered.

Hamhock nodded halfheartedly and gave the young mammoth a pat.

Stony came in with Froggy perched on his shoulder. The frog eyed the dodo meat with distaste, but the boy sat right down and began gnawing on some gnarly unidentifiable organ. Echo whipped out some equally nasty vegetable and began to break it into bite-sized bits. We were soon surrounded by a buzzing little cloud of fruit flies.

"The cold seems to affect the strangest things," I said. "There were never this many flies before."

"It is a little weird," said Echo, crunching on a bit of vegetable.

"Speaking of pests," I said, "I think I've found out how Bonehead and Bugeyes wormed their way back into the clan."

Stony looked up and loudly swallowed whatever it was he was chewing.

"Chip," I explained, "overheard them telling Boulder that they actually *had* killed me in the jungle. I guess they figured I'd never come back, so he'd never find out."

"But what *I* don't get," said Echo, "is why Boulder wanted to bump you off in the first place. I mean, yes, you're a pain in the—"

"According to Chip," I interrupted, "Boulder is worried that I could be the next Big Man instead of his son. *Crazy*, huh?"

"Why is that crazy?" she asked.

"Come on, Echo. I'm the smallest kid in my clan. I have about as much chance of becoming the next Big Man as you do."

A mischievous smile spread slowly across her face. "Then you might have a better shot than you think," she said.

I noticed her bright green eyes get all twinkly and suddenly found it hard to argue with her. Girls are annoying.

\|\|\|\|\|

*BAM! BAM! BAM!* came the rhythmic banging of stones as Boulder led our procession through the jungle toward Headstone Field. Each player marched in front of a very unhappy-looking jungle llama, pulling the animal by its short trunk. First came Boulder and the older players, in order of their steeds' sizes. Next came this year's rookies, led by Bonehead. Finally, leading Woolly by his trunk, Stony and I brought up the rear. To prevent their clan from spotting them, Echo and Hamhock walked underneath Woolly, hidden by long, shaggy curtains of mammoth hair.

I had watched a few Big Games before, but it felt very different to be a player. My heart raced as we rounded the base of Mount Bigbigbig and saw the great Headstone Field ahead. Under a crisp blue sky, two crowds waited for us on opposite sidelines. On the left were the women, girls, and youngest boys of my clan. They cheered wildly as the first of our players stepped out of the jungle and onto the field. On the right was a strikingly similar crowd of Boar Rider supporters, hissing like a pit full of angry snakes. Although the sun was now at its peak in the sky, the air felt scarcely warmer than it had at night, and I could see strange clouds in the far distance—higher and lighter than any I'd ever seen.

*BAM! BAM! BAM!* came the rhythmic banging from the opposite side of the field. A procession of mud-painted Boar Riders stepped out of the distant trees, leading their fierce razorback boars by their tusks. Their fans whooped and whistled, while our side booed deafeningly.

Because of Woolly's position at the back of the procession, he was still hidden from the crowds by the trees. Stony was standing awkwardly, like he needed to pee.

"Go in those bushes," I whispered. "You still have time."

He shook his head resolutely.

Boss Hog led Big Mumma toward the center of the field as the squads each waited on their end. I watched the huge sow plod along, the Shiny Stone on her back. When they reached the middle of the field, Boss Hog eased the Shiny Stone off her and planted it on the ground. It shone, slightly, in the noonday sun.

A clan could win the Big Game only by getting the Shiny Stone to their side of the field. There were many more rules, but no one ever followed them, mainly because if someone stopped and brought up a rule, someone else whacked him in the head with a rock.

Boss Hog scanned the ground around him and chose the largest rock he could palm. Then he climbed onto Big Mumma's back. "Boar Riders mount!" he commanded.

Stony started doing the pee-pee dance—holding his gourd and jumping up and down.

"Go already!" I said.

He ran off into the bushes.

On our end of the field, Boulder the Bountiful stepped forward and chose the heaviest hunk of granite he could lift. "Macrauchenia Riders, mount!" he barked.

I climbed up Woolly's side until I felt a hand grab me and yank me back down. "No, Little Slug," said Bonehead, brandishing the club my father had given me. *"Me* ride boarauchenia."

"Don't be stupid," I said. "You don't even—"

He slammed the club into my chest.

I doubled over and fell, gasping for breath.

The brute clutched a handful of Woolly's hair and clambered up onto the mammoth's back. "Boy with biggest beast next Big Man!" he shouted down to me. Then he grabbed Woolly by the ears and pulled hard. "Go, beast!"

Yelping in pain, the young mammoth charged out of the trees and onto the field.

"Charge that Piggyback!" cried Bonehead, pointing at Boss Hog and yanking on Woolly's right ear.

A hush descended over the Boar Riders and their crowd as they caught sight of the mammoth for the first time. Boss Hog, normally a healthy pinkish hue, turned as pale as a pork chop. "Back, Big Mumma!" he cried. "Back!"

"CHARGE!" cried Boulder, eager to press the sudden advantage his son had created. "Macrauchenia Riders, CHARGE!"

And most of them did charge. And our clan's

supporters cheered. And I continued to writhe on the ground in pain.

It was Hamhock who stepped up this time. He had seen Bonehead bash me and—as the brute had climbed up Woolly's side—Hamhock had taken action. A diehard Boar Riders' fan, he had jumped out from under the mammoth and whispered something in Woolly's ear.

Now, just as Woolly reached the middle of the field, Bonehead found himself unexpectedly hurtling through the air, flapping his arms and shrieking like a dodo bird.

Woolly had listened to Hamhock and bucked hard.

The Boar Rider fans shouted their approval.

Echo ran over to me. "Are you okay?" she asked.

"Yeah." I nodded, and pointed. "But this does not look good for Woolly."

Seeing their secret weapon buck, Boulder and the other Macrauchenia Riders had halted their charge and were standing around, gaping.

Boss Hog took the opportunity to swing Big Mumma back around. "BOAR RIDERS," he bellowed. "SHOW OUR MIGHT!"

And they charged. And their crowd roared. And the Macrauchenia Riders scattered. Chip was the first one down, bonked in the back by Newporker. Rock was next—whacked by Oinker. The Boar Rider fans cheered wildly and began to sing their fight song:

*When Big Game comes*
*and time to fight,*
*we kick your bums*

*and show our might!*
*Turn Llama's Boys*
*to pile o' bones,*
*and always KEEEEEP . . .*
*great Shiny Stone!*

Now, I couldn't care less about the Shiny Stone, but the sight of my dad being chased by the snarling, stone-wielding Snortimer was making my blood boil. I caught up to Woolly on the edge of the field and mounted. Both crowds went berserk as Woolly and I charged back into the fray.

"That one!" I cried, pointing at the closest Boar Rider, who happened to be Boss Hog's son, Baconbits.

Woolly reached out with his trunk and yanked the scowling boy off his squealing boar.

"Into that one!" I said, pointing at Snortimer, who was about to bash my dad.

Woolly flung Baconbits across the field like a jiggling water skin.

"Boar's-eye!" yelled our supporters as Snortimer toppled to the ground, out cold.

"That's my boy!" cheered my dad.

Watching Snortimer get knocked out scared a few of the Boar Riders right off the field. Boss Hog grabbed Baconbits and waddled after them. The remaining Boar Riders looked unsure about what to do. I decided to make their decision easier.

Seeing the mammoth barreling toward them, the last of the Boar Riders turned tail and ran screaming, several of them crashing into one another. Our fans began to sing:

*On Big Game day*
*it's Llama Time!*
*So run away,*
*you silly swine!*
*Crush Piggybacks*
*until they MOAAAAAAAN,*
*and then bring back*
*great Shiny Stone!*

Stony ran toward the center of the field as the last of the Boar Riders fled into the jungle. While the crowd belted out the fight song over and over, Stony single-handedly dragged the Shiny Stone toward their outstretched arms. I watched in amazement as two girls actually ran onto the field and kissed him. He turned and winked at me.

I glanced at Echo. She was petting Woolly and could not have looked more pleased. Our plan had worked. It was the shortest Big Game anyone could remember, but we had won it for the Macrauchenia Riders and would be allowed back into the clan.

"Lug and Stony!" went up the triumphant cry among our teammates. "Stony and Lug!" They lifted us onto their shoulders and did a joyful dance called the Macrauchenia. The entire crowd joined in.

\\|||/

Woolly carried the Shiny Stone to the village and went to rest in the big drafty cavern around back. Everyone else busied themselves with preparations for the great victory feast. Well, everyone except Stony and me. We were given places of honor on top of the newly installed Shiny Stone in the public clearing.

"Bring Echo and Hamhock up here too," I commanded.

And people actually did it!

Chip started drumming on Rock's head. Froggy began bobbing rhythmically on Stony's shoulder. Stony joined in, arching his unibrow to the beat. People started to dance. There is no doubt that it would have been the most rocking party of the Stone Age but for the sudden blood-chilling scream that pierced the air.

# ☰ 13 ☰

# A QUESTION OF TRUST

**I JOINED THE** crowd running toward the other side of the village and stopped when I saw Bugeyes lying on the ground just outside Woolly's cavern. Then I spotted the two puncture wounds in the boy's backside. They were the same size and distance apart as those I'd seen in the severed boar's head. Bugeyes was faint with loss of blood, and his father, Frogface, was trying to stanch the bleeding by covering the wounds with leaves. Bonehead stood staring down at his wounded friend in slack-jawed disbelief. I glanced up at the cavern and saw one anxious mammoth eye peering out. This was not looking good.

"Your fault!" Frogface screamed at me. "Your nasty boarauchenia attacked my son!"

I opened my mouth, but nothing came out.

"We're truly sorry about your son," said Echo, stepping forward. "But Woolly would never do something like this."

"Stinking Piggyback!" Bonehead snarled. "Shut mouth!"

"Hey!" Hamhock piped up, drawing himself up to his full four feet and puffing out his chest. "That's my sister!"

Bonehead shook a fist at the kid. "Me crack little—"

"If you touch him," Echo warned, "I'll—"

"Silence!" barked Boulder, stepping out of the crowd. "SILENCE!"

Everyone stopped talking and watched the Big Man walk around the semiconscious Bugeyes. He made a show of examining the two puncture wounds and glancing darkly in Woolly's direction. On his second time around,

Boulder stopped directly in front of me, his look suggesting I was a pile of pig poo that he'd accidentally stepped in.

"Let me guess," I said. "You want us to leave?"

"No, you can stay," he said with a chilling calmness in his voice. Then he pointed at Woolly. "*If* you kill your boarauchenia."

I stared at him, feeling nauseous. "And if we don't?"

"Go with your Piggyback friends," he said, gesturing toward Echo and Hamhock. "If you don't bother us again, we won't bother you."

I looked from Boulder to the rest of the crowd. I saw my family on the other side of the throng, watching me with stunned faces. I looked over at Woolly. I was sure he wouldn't attack an innocent person, but Bugeyes was not exactly innocent— maybe he'd thrown rocks at Woolly or done something equally stupid.

Echo was shaking her head as if she were reading my thoughts. "Woolly didn't do this," she whispered. "He's not vicious."

I glanced at the young mammoth, then at Echo

and Hamhock again. They were now banished from both tribes and would have nowhere to go. Stony was already standing with them. I turned back to Boulder. "I'll go with them," I said.

The Big Man looked smug—as if he'd just made a big bet and won. "All right, Lug," he said. "Your choice."

\|\|\|\|\|

I didn't look at my family as I left. I knew that if I did, I wouldn't be able to go. As the sun descended, my friends and I led Woolly back through the jungle to the big red cavern by the creek. For the rest of the evening, the young mammoth just lay there, staring straight ahead, his huge brown eyes resembling nothing more than empty caves.

"He's so traumatized that he won't even communicate," Echo whispered to me. "I'm sure he saw whomever attacked Bugeyes."

The gusting wind keened through the cave that night, biting into my flesh as I tried to fall asleep. I thought about how strange life was. Just when you thought your biggest problem was solved, something even more colossal happened. What was it that Crazy Crag had said? There's always something bigger coming around the mountain? Maybe he wasn't so crazy after all.

I was dozing off when Stony nudged me awake to take the night's last watch. I sat next to Woolly and watched the pale reddish dawn light bleed out of the horizon. Every feature of the landscape stood out in stark silhouette. I stared at the jagged cliffs and the fingerlike outcropping that marked my secret art cave—always beckoning. Woolly's hollow eyes drew me back. What kind of monster had this poor creature seen? Whatever it was, I had a sinking feeling that Bugeyes wouldn't be the last victim. I looked back out at the silhouetted cliffs. Suddenly, I had an idea.

"Rise and shine, everyone," I said. "Rise and shine!"

Hamhock sat up and rubbed the sleep from his eyes. Echo somehow managed to glower at me with her eyes still closed. Stony and Froggy kept right on snoring.

"Wake them up!" I said to Hamhock as I ran out of the cave into the dawn light. "I'll be right back."

||||/

I crawled through a pitch-black tunnel, the familiar scent of dank limestone like sweet perfume to my nose. Moving by feel, I turned left at the first fork, then right, then right again. I heard a loud scampering noise behind me and wondered if it was a big tunnel rat. After a while, I glimpsed a thin shaft of sunlight in the passageway ahead. I climbed through an opening above me and stood up in a spacious oval chamber. Its vaulted ceiling was dotted by myriad sunlit holes that dappled the floor with a stunning sprinkling of light.

On the walls were paintings of my family, of other clan folk, of raucous weddings, of somber burials, of peaceful jungle llamas, of nervous-looking dodos, and of every other beautiful bird and beast that I had found in the forest. An entire wall was devoted to paintings of my father and me doing things together, including one of us painting together. Of course, making art was strictly forbidden "uncaveman-like behavior," and my father would have never painted with me. But seeing this made me feel like it *could* happen someday. All of my art was here in one place—the secret fruit of years of cultivation, careful craft, and hard labor.

I walked over to my most recent painting—a bare gourd tree. It was something I'd been working on since I'd noticed the trees losing all their leaves. Beneath that half-finished artwork lay my pigment rocks—red ocher, yellow ocher, lime white, and umber. I sat down beside them and considered how it would feel to remain in my cave and forget all my troubles—to work on my art and not bother with the rest of the world. I couldn't resist picking up the yellow ocher and crushing a bit of it in my hand. The powder was such a vivid color, so much more beautiful than the dusty gray of the caves where I spent most of my time.

Then I thought of Stony and Echo and Hamhock, and even injured Bugeyes. I felt like I needed other people—needed their help and needed to help them, maybe even more than I needed my paintings. I picked up the other pigment rocks, tucked them into my leaf sash, and headed back out of the cave.

Stony, Echo, and Hamhock were already up and waiting for me. Woolly was still sprawled on the floor, staring blankly at a wall. I walked over to him and offered him the rocks that I'd brought.

"Woolly," I said, "would you show us what happened to Bugeyes yesterday?"

The young mammoth eyed the colored lumps but did not move.

"It might save someone else from being hurt."

Woolly looked at me for a long time. Slowly, laboriously, he got to his feet. He grasped the yellow ocher rock with the tip of his trunk and raised it to the cave wall. Then he began to draw.

At first we all agreed that Woolly was drawing a yellow cat with a rat in its mouth. Then Woolly gave the rat bulging eyes and the cat two incredibly long teeth. He made the two canine teeth long enough to skewer the rat.

"Is that . . . Bugeyes?" asked Echo, pointing at the ratlike figure.

Woolly nodded.

"Okay," I said, pointing at the catlike figure large enough to hold Bugeyes in its mouth. "What is that thing, then?"

An ominous purring sound emanated from the back of the cave.

I whipped around and gasped. A monstrous

feline with shining golden eyes emerged from the darkness. The giant cat moved sinuously—massive muscles rolling beneath thick tan-and-black-striped fur. He stopped directly in front of me and made a complicated sound that was half hiss, half roar.

I stared, mesmerized, at his foot-long saber teeth—extending far down past his chin—streaked with dried blood.

He made the same vocalization again.

*Focus on the sound*, I thought, my eyes still locked on his hideous teeth. *On the sound.*

And the meaning of the cat's message soon became clear. "My name," he was saying, "is Smilus."

# ⊜ 14 ⊜

# SMILUS

**"W-W-WHAT . . . ARE YOU?"** I stammered.

Before Smilus could answer, Woolly dropped the yellow ocher rock with a *thud*, his ears flapping wide. He tilted his head so that the tips of his tusks were pointing directly at the cat's throat.

Smilus looked at the young mammoth. "Hello, Woolly," he said.

"You two . . . know each other?" I asked.

"Oh yes," replied Smilus. "Woolly's clan and we saber-toothed cats go way back."

The young mammoth stomped a threatening

foot, and the cavern echoed with the sound. I glanced around surreptitiously until I spotted a sharp rock on the floor. But before I could even stoop down, the cat batted it away with lightning speed. It shattered against the wall, just below Woolly's drawing.

"Don't want to damage the lovely picture of me and the boy," said Smilus. "I think it sends the right message."

We all glanced at the drawing of Smilus attacking Bugeyes. Echo cleared her throat. "And what message is that?"

"Hamela, isn't it?"

She stared, stunned.

"*Ham . . . ela,*" he whispered, as if tasting her name. "I've been watching you for quite a while now. I enjoyed one of your clan's boars the other day. Afterward, I watched your little friend Lug here stumble upon its head." He smiled at me and exposed the bloodred gums from which his saber teeth emerged.

I shuddered. This beast must have been silently stalking us for days.

He looked from Echo to me. "If your clans don't want to suffer the same fate," he hissed, "they'd best abandon their caves and go elsewhere."

There was a long, shocked silence.

"Where would they go?" I finally asked.

"If they know what's good for them, far, far away."

"But why? I mean . . . this forest has enough food for all of us!"

"Stupid boy," said Smilus. "The world is changing. I'm just the tip of the iceberg."

"What's an iceberg?" Hamhock whispered to Echo.

The cat's eyes glittered with cruel amusement. "You fools have no idea what's going on, do you?" He nodded toward Mount Bigbigbig. "Haven't you looked out from the top of your own little hill?"

"Mount Bigbigbig is sacred," said Echo. "No one's allowed up there."

Smilus sneered. "Time to open your eyes. That bug-eyed boy was just a little taste of what's to come." He sauntered silently out of the cavern and then turned back. "I will give your people until tomorrow's sunrise to get out of their caves. Or no one will see sunset."

I watched him disappear into the morning mist between the trees as the jungle around him fell eerily silent.

# ⊜ 15 ⊜

# BIG BIG BIG

**"COME ON, HAMELA,"** Hamhock whined as the sounds of the jungle slowly resumed. *"Pleeeeease."* He was watching his sister climb up onto Woolly's back.

"No, Hamhock," she said, "you'll be safer here."

Echo and I had immediately agreed on a plan, and there was not a moment to waste. "Time to open our eyes," I said, leading Woolly out of the cave.

Hamhock dashed toward us, but Stony scooped him up and held him.

Before he could whine again, Echo and I were out of the cave and thundering through the jungle on the Woolly Mammoth Express.

"Lug?" whispered Echo as we approached the looming mountain.

"Yeah?"

"Are you nervous about climbing Mount Bigbigbig?"

"No," I said. "I'm nervous about never coming back down."

She tittered anxiously.

"Did you feel that?" I asked.

"Cold rain?" guessed Echo, looking up at the treetops whizzing by.

It was only when Woolly began to climb the slope of the mountain and the jungle canopy gave way to bigger patches of sky that we saw the strange white flakes coming down.

"They're beautiful!" cried Echo.

"They turn to water when you touch them!" I said.

She laughed in delight as the white flakes melted on her upturned face.

Woolly made a deep rumbling sound that sounded like *SNOOOOOOOOOW*.

"What?" I said.

"That must be what mammoths call this stuff!" shouted Echo over the wind.

The snow came down faster as we climbed higher. The wind gusted and wailed, lifting the strange white stuff off the ground so that the whole landscape seemed ghostly.

"How close are we?" shouted Echo.

"I'm not sure," I said, squinting through the flurry of flakes.

Echo looked around and shivered. "Do you think it might be true what they say?"

"About the mountain?"

"About the ghosts of the banished," she said, "wandering around, looking for the clan folk that exiled them?"

"I don't know about ghosts," I said, pointing across the slope. "But I'd bet my life that's Crazy Crag's cave over there."

We both gazed at a little opening in a distant ridge. "Lug," said Echo, "why is the cave's mouth flickering like that?"

"I think it's a trick of the eyes—from all the snowflakes dancing in front of us."

She snuggled deeper into Woolly's fur. "When Crazy Crag invited you up there . . . were you tempted to go?"

"Do I look crazy to you?"

She didn't reply.

"He just jumped out of nowhere, cackled something about beasts and storm light, and told me to come up for a visit."

We stared some more at the falling snow and

the strange flickering cave. "So I guess you know the legend about him?" she asked.

"You mean the part about how he can turn his hands into bolts of storm light and strike down anyone who comes near him?"

"Yes," she said, "that part."

"That's why we won't be stopping by his place anytime soon," I replied.

Then I pointed up the mountain and Woolly charged up another long stretch of steep slope. He seemed very much at home in the snow—as if he'd been made for moving through it.

〜〜〜

As we crested the peak of Mount Bigbigbig, I looked out over the vista to the north. The most astounding sight met my eyes. An enormous herd of strange beasts was slowly making its way toward the mountain across the great white snow-covered plain below. It was like watching an entire ant colony on the move, although from their gait these appeared to be large hoofed creatures. There were several other immense herds farther back, but I couldn't tell much about them at this distance. Then I noticed some closer but smaller packs of animals. I could make out some lumbering giant slothlike beasts, which seemed to periodically rear up on two legs. Just in front of them were shaggy creatures sporting antlers like upturned giants' hands. I glanced over at Woolly and followed his gaze to a herd of woolly mammoths that was just starting to lumber up the north slope of the mountain.

Woolly flapped his ears, lifted his trunk, and trumpeted jubilantly.

"It's his family!" cried Echo.

I patted Woolly's head. "I'm happy for you," I whispered to him.

"Lug!" said Echo. "Look in that grove." She pointed to a dark stand of dead trees behind the mammoth herd.

I followed her finger, squinting, until I saw movement. And there they were, among the twisted tree trunks, a huge pride of saber-toothed tigers slinking their way through the shadows.

"Stone it!" I muttered. "That's a lot of cats."

"Lug, do you have any idea what's going on here?"

"I'm not sure," I said. "But I think all these creatures are following the cold snow from the north."

"But . . . why would anyone follow the cold?"

I touched Woolly's thick shaggy hair. "Remember how warm it was sleeping next to him?"

She nodded.

"Now imagine if your entire body was completely covered by hair like that."

"How charming," she muttered. "I . . . guess I'd be too hot."

"Right," I said. "You'd be too hot, unless—"

"Unless it was getting colder and colder!"

"Exactly. And all these northern creatures have thick coats. I think they can only live where it's cold."

She looked out over the great snow-covered northern plain. "So . . . as the cold spreads from north to south . . . it opens up new foraging territory for them?"

"Or, if you're a meat eater, new hunting grounds."

"Right," she said. "And if there aren't any people around, the cats won't need to compete with us for boars . . . or caves to shelter in—"

"Or jungle llamas," I said, suddenly remembering. "The day before Stony and I were banished, a macrauchenia mysteriously disappeared from our village stable. Everyone blamed it on your clan, but I'd bet anything it was Smilus."

Woolly slowly knelt on the ground—a signal for us to dismount. We did so and found ourselves ankle deep in the snow.

"Hey . . . Woolly?" said Echo. *"Woolly!"*

But he was already barreling down the hillside.

We watched him run as the saber-toothed cats crept toward his herd.

"He's going to warn his family," she said.

I nodded. "We'd better do the same."

# ◈ 16 ◈

# DAWN OF THE ICE AGE

**TRAVEL IS MUCH** slower when you don't have a mammoth, but we did manage to get down the mountainside before dark. The snow had not yet reached the base of the mountain, and Echo ran for her village as I raced to pick up Stony and Hamhock.

"What happened here?" I cried, seeing both boys sprawled on the floor of the red cavern.

"Bonehead," said Hamhock, sitting up against the wall and gingerly rubbing his backside.

Stony sat up and grunted in agreement. He

had a nasty bruise around his unibrow.

"I can't believe this!" I shouted. "Boulder promised they'd leave us alone if we left the village."

"But me didn't," said Bonehead, suddenly darkening the entrance. He was still gripping the club my father had given me.

"What do you want from us?" I cried.

He grinned and pointed out of the cave. Behind him, Boulder was leading the men of the Macrauchenia Rider Council toward us.

I strode out of the cave and waved at the councilmen. "I'm glad you're all here," I declared. "I've got some really important news, and—"

I stopped talking and looked around. They were all eyeing me suspiciously.

"*What?*" I asked.

Boulder stepped forward. "You tell us, *Loony Lug.*"

"Loony . . . ? What? Right now—as we squabble like dodos—there are giant cats making their way toward our village."

A few councilmen snickered.

I swallowed my pride and continued. "There are all kinds of beasts migrating this way, following the cold. There's a great storm of white flakes coming."

"Uh-oh," said Boulder to the councilmen, "Loony Lug is at it again!"

The laughter spread.

"Climb the mountain and see for yourselves!" I said.

The laughs turned to gasps.

"*So,*" said Boulder, looming over me, "you broke our law and climbed our sacred mountain!"

I took a deep breath. "Why is *only* the mountain sacred?" I asked.

Boulder's eyes narrowed. "What?"

"Why isn't the ground we're standing on sacred too? We couldn't live without it."

"What are you babbling about, *Loony*?"

"I'm saying that everything in our jungle is sacred, including us, and we need to protect ourselves before it's too late. The giant cat that attacked Bugeyes said that if—" I stopped again. I could see that no one believed a word I was saying.

Boulder pointed at the drawing of Smilus attacking Bugeyes. "Did the 'giant cat' make this?" he asked sarcastically.

"No," I said. "Woolly did."

*"Woolly?"* The Big Man sneered. "And did *Woolly* paint your secret art cave?" he asked, pointing at the fingerlike outcropping in the distance.

I stared at him, speechless. I had never told anyone about my art cave. How did Boulder know?

Then I saw Bonehead's smug little smile. "Me saw Little Slug crawl in," he said. "Me follow."

"I thought I heard a rat," I said.

"Me tell everyone," he said, his smile growing.

From the looks on the men's faces, I had a feeling that they had gone in and seen all my paintings—each one a violation of clan law. I closed my eyes and took a deep breath.

But instead of feeling small and ashamed, I remembered how the painting of my family had started my friendship with Woolly. And how the mammoth's last drawing had revealed Bugeyes's attacker. I thought about everything art had taught me—observation, focus, persistence, even courage. How creating something new with my hands had always sent shivers down my spine. I opened my eyes and looked back at the men. "I'm a cave painter," I said. "And no law is going to change that."

They stared at me in silence.

"And no law," I continued, "should prevent us from joining together to try to survive the big changes coming."

Frogface stepped forward from the group of councilmen. "If what you're saying *were* true, we would have to change *everything*," he said.

I nodded hopefully.

"So you're obviously nuts!" he concluded.

"Crazy as Crag!" declared Boulder.

The other councilmen began to nod in agreement.

Then Bonehead laughed at something behind me. I turned and saw a bruised Stony and Hamhock limp out of the red cavern.

"Look!" Bonehead said. "Loony Lug's big fans! Why them all beat-up, Loony?"

Boulder smirked too, clearly admiring his son's handiwork.

I turned to my friends. "Let's go," I said.

〽〡〡〡〢

By the time we got to our prearranged meeting spot by the dead tree, Echo was already waiting.

"Please tell me you had more luck than we did," I said.

She shook her head. "They thought I was a traitor trying to get them to leave their caves so that your clan could take over their territory. One councilman suggested they put me in the Tiny Dark Cave."

"Let me guess," I said. "Snortimer?"

She nodded sadly.

"Well, as my mom likes to say, there's a dingleberry in every bush."

"Yeah," said Echo. "Too bad that dingleberry's my father."

I stared at her. I remembered Snortimer's red hair and green eyes and saw a faint resemblance. But that was where the similarity ended. Then I thought about Bonehead and Boulder. I was amazed that someone with a father like Snortimer could turn out like Echo. "Your mom must be really nice," I said.

"I don't really remember her," said Echo. "She died after giving birth to my brother."

"Oh." I wanted to give her a hug but found myself staring at my feet instead.

"Anyway," she said, "I managed to catch a ride before they caught me." She nodded toward the stupendous snout now emerging from behind the dead tree.

Froggy gave an exultant croak and hopped off Stony's shoulder onto Big Mumma's delighted face—showering her with slimy-tongued frog kisses.

"But that's Boss Hog's personal boar!" Hamhock piped up.

"Exactly," said Echo, mounting Big Mumma.

"Hold on a moment," I said. "What's your plan?"

Echo arched an eyebrow and put a finger to her lips.

Suddenly, I too heard the very low rumble of hoofbeats.

"Please don't tell me that's all the Boar Riders coming for you," I muttered.

"Okay, I won't," she said. "But we should probably get going."

# ⊜ 17 ⊜

# HOG WILD

**I FOUND PIGGYBACKING** much scarier than mammoth riding. Despite four human passengers and a frog, Big Mumma ran fast and furious—snout-plowing through thick foliage and even leaping over a creek as the pursuing Boar Riders nipped at her hooves.

After much cringing, ducking, and a good deal of terrified screaming, we approached my village. I ducked as Big Mumma charged under a low-hanging gourd tree and leapt into the public clearing, snorting to a halt just in front of the Shiny Stone. The Boar Riders followed suit. Soon Boss Hog, Snortimer, and a dozen other angry men on pigs surrounded us. The enormous Boss Hog looked particularly annoyed to be on a smaller sow than ours. His animal didn't look too happy either.

The Macrauchenia Riders emerged from their caves and headed toward us, led by Boulder.

"Echo," I muttered, "I *really* hope you have a plan."

"Already happening," she whispered. "Welcome to the first-ever Joint Clan Conference!"

"WHAT'S THIS?" Boulder barked at Boss Hog. "Why are you on my land, *llama thief?*"

"*Me?*" said Boss Hog, working his pink jowls into a lather and pointing at us. "Your spies stole MY BOAR!"

"They're not MY SPIES!"

"YES THEY ARE!"

"NO THEY'RE NOT!"

"YES THEY ARE!"

"NO THEY'RE NOT!"

"Great plan," I whispered to Echo.

She shot me a withering look. "Do you have a better idea?"

"You mean better than listening to those two yell?"

"We just need to get them to realize that they face a much bigger threat than each other."

"That would take a miracle," I muttered.

A snowflake fluttered down from the sky and melted on my forehead.

Echo smiled.

"Huh?" said Boss Hog, peering up at the hazy late afternoon sky.

"What's this white stuff?" muttered Boulder.

"Woolly calls it *snow*," said Echo. "Well, *snooooooooow*."

He ignored her.

I cleared my throat and turned to Boulder. "Remember the great storm I mentioned today? And the giant cats following the cold?"

Boulder looked like a dodo bird spotting the club that's about to whack him.

Boss Hog looked at Echo with a similar expression. "It's . . . all true?" he asked, his voice quavering.

She nodded.

Boulder closed his mouth and gulped. "When do the giant cats come?"

"Tomorrow," I said. "Sunrise."

|||||

In the Council Circle clearing just outside our village, I stood and listened intently to the first-ever Joint Clan Council.

"Don't you see?" shouted Snortimer at his fellow Boar Rider councilmen. "This could all be some dirty Macrauchenia Riders' trick to destroy our way of life! These Llama's Boys hate our way of life!" He was saying this while shivering, as the snow piled on his own head.

When Boss Hog pointed this out, Snortimer snorted loudly and stormed off into the forest. I shook my head in amazement. It seemed that no amount of evidence was enough for some people.

"Boss Hog," I said, "can we talk in private?"

The Big Man growled dismissively and pointed

at his own head. "I've got some big thinking to do!"

"Well, I have a big thought for keeping the giant cats away," I said. "At least for a while."

"You?" he half laughed. "But you're . . . *little*."

"I'm aware of that," I said. "But as my mother likes to say, sometimes big dodos grow out of small eggs."

Boss Hog looked confused but grudgingly followed me out of the circle.

When we were out of earshot of the council, I stopped and turned to him. "Okay," I said, "what is the one thing we humans have that giant cats don't?"

He stared blankly at me. "I've never seen a giant cat."

"Any cats, then."

He scratched his forehead and shrugged.

"Hands!" I said. "They have paws, but we have hands. And that means we can throw things."

He looked down at his own ham-sized mitts and furrowed his brow. "We throw giant cats?" he asked hopefully.

"No! We throw stones!"

A big childlike grin spread across his face. "I like to throw stones!"

"Good," I said. "I want you to tell everyone to start gathering stones and piling them in each cave entrance. Then, at sunrise tomorrow, whenever a cat approaches one of our caves, the headstone players in the surrounding caves will pelt him."

The Big Man still looked confused.

"We'll throw stones," I clarified. "At cats."

He nodded. "Good plan."

"Not really," I admitted. "But at least it will give us some time to keep thinking. Also, we need to make sure everyone stays as warm as possible. Echo is working on that problem and—"

But Boss Hog was already waddling back to the Council Circle to present the throwing stones idea as his own.

彳彳彳

Under the light of a thin ghostly moon, we all gathered stones. Echo pointed out that it would be much easier to work together and defend everyone in a single village, so Boss Hog sent Oinker and Newporker to bring the rest of their clan. She also pointed out that the more people gathered in the same caves, the warmer they could remain.

The snow slowly piled up in the public clearing, and the mounds of stones grew steadily taller in every cave entrance until they were halfway up to the ceilings.

At the first hint of dawn, everyone hurried inside. Most went toward the back of the caves, but Echo, Stony, and I and all of the headstone players positioned ourselves behind the various stone piles. Then we waited.

It wasn't long before the chirping and buzzing of the morning forest went suddenly and uncannily silent. Without so much as a rustle, Smilus stalked out of the trees into the clearing. Every step he took, every motion he made, seemed effortlessly graceful, and I found myself wanting to paint him. Instead, I quietly picked up a stone from the nearby pile. Next to me, Echo and Stony did the same.

A dozen tigers slunk into the clearing after Smilus—their yellow, foot-long saber teeth glinting in the first rays of morning sun.

Smilus surveyed the humans in the caves. "*Mmmmmmm*," he purred. "Looks like everyone's staying for breakfast."

The largest tigress licked her chops. Her cold green eyes were locked on Boss Hog, who was quivering like a bowl of lard in the leftmost cave. "That pink round one looks nice and juicy," she hissed.

"He's all yours," said Smilus, turning toward us. "I'll be starting out with these three bite-sized morsels."

"And I've got dibs on that hairy one!" growled a cat with an extra-long left saber tooth and oddly crooked black stripes. He was ogling a quaking Boulder in the rightmost cave.

"Sure," said Smilus. "Enjoy."

A few of the other cats called out their choices. One licked his lips in my dad's direction. Another salivated at the sight of Snortimer. And a buff young beast crunched his teeth at Bonehead.

"All right," said Smilus, "it's breakfast ti—" He jumped back and snarled as my stone whizzed by him.

I swore under my breath.

Smilus's eyes narrowed to black slits. Without a word, he leapt toward our cave.

*Wap! Wap!* A rapid volley thumped him left and right. Smilus took a couple of quick surprised steps backward. Stony and Echo grinned at each other and slapped hands.

Now the tigress sprang forward. *Wap!* A little

stone bounced off her snout. She drew back.

"Chew on that, kitty!" shouted Hamhock, who had snuck up to our rock pile from the back of the cave where he was supposed to be.

And so it went for every cat: a leap forward, a volley of stones, a step or two backward.

But still—slowly, inexorably, the beasts crept toward the caves.

Soon, Smilus was close enough that I could see his oily hairs bristling. He smirked at me when he saw that there were no more rocks in our pile.

I stepped backward, wiping the sweat from my eyes.

"No need to wipe it away, Lug," he said. "I like my humans nice and salty."

Suddenly, I saw his left saber tooth splinter with a sickening crack. Echo had thrown the last stone in her hand. The tiger's golden eyes blazed with fury.

*"Ladies first, then!"* he hissed, leaping at her.

"No!" I cried, stepping between them.

# ⊜ 18 ⊜

# LADIES FIRST

SOMETHING BIG AND snakelike suddenly lunged into the cave and wrapped itself around Smilus's neck.

One moment the cat was a hairbreadth from me—teeth bared—and the next he was dangling in the air outside the cave.

"Mm . . . Mm . . . Mam?" he stammered.

"That's right," said a deep, rumbling voice. "Remember me?"

I scampered over to the cave entrance and looked up. A colossal reddish-brown mammoth had her trunk wrapped around the pop-eyed cat. Woolly was next to her—less than half the size of his mother, but scowling at Smilus just as fiercely. A dozen other mammoths were facing off with tigers around the clearing.

"What about Woolly's father?" Mam demanded, bringing the squirming Smilus eye to eye with her. "Remember him?"

The big cat gasped for breath.

Suddenly, the tigress left Boss Hog and leapt at Mam, clawing a thick mat of fur off her left front leg with a terrible ripping sound.

Mam dropped Smilus, who landed on the tigress. Both cats yelped and staggered backward. The other mammoths charged. The cats leapt. The clearing echoed with roars, snarls, and yelps of pain.

Soon three tigers had Woolly surrounded.

"You pathetic hairball," hissed Smilus. "Ready to die like your daddy?"

The mammoths were bigger and stronger, but the cats were more nimble and ruthless. They didn't think twice about attacking the herd's smallest and weakest.

Mam came rumbling toward them—scattering cats left and right.

They regrouped and ganged up on an old tusk-less mammoth called Glacier. But it soon became clear that as long as Mam was around, the cats could never hold an advantage for very long.

Finally, six tigers trapped her against a cave wall, while the other six kept the remaining mammoths at bay.

Smilus crouched to leap for her exposed neck. "Any last words?" he sneered.

She looked around wild-eyed, but she was completely surrounded.

"Okay, Mam, time to say good-bYEOWWW-WWWWWWW!" Smilus shrieked, feeling a tusk where no tusk should ever be felt.

He hightailed it into the trees as Woolly charged down the line, tusking every tiger butt in his path. Five more cats yowled and followed their boss into the jungle. Seeing their number cut in half, the rest disappeared just as quickly as they'd come.

At first, no one moved. We waited in our caves,

listening. Had we really just been saved from certain death by a herd of shaggy behemoths? The four of us dashed out and hugged Woolly.

Soon, the other kids followed, gazing up in awe at the great beasts. Next came the women, shouting for the children to be careful. Finally, the men emerged, calling enthusiastically for a victory feast.

Unfortunately, the party would have to wait. We soon heard savage voices above us and saw the cats in the bare branches of the large gourd trees that surrounded our village.

Smilus's big sinister eyes met mine. "Just wait until nightfall," he hissed. "All you've done is delayed your own funeral."

I looked at the sky and remembered last night's tiny sliver of a moon. "If they come down tonight," I said to Mam, "we won't be able to see them."

Mam nodded gravely. "They killed Woolly's father on a moonless night."

Echo glanced at Woolly, who was staring up at the treetops. "Mam," she said, "is that when your son got separated from the herd?"

"A moon's turn ago," said the matriarch, "as

we were heading south, the cats attacked us and killed Woolly's father. My son got lost trying to run after them in the dark."

"You!" shouted Boulder, pointing at Echo through the crowd. "You can talk to those . . . mammoth things, right?"

Echo's eyes narrowed, but she nodded.

"Well, talk to that boss mammoth there," he said, pointing at Mam. "They need to shake those trees and get rid of those cats now!"

Echo turned to Mam, but she had already understood.

"It's not so easy," said Echo, interpreting Mam's words. "If we shake those trees, the cats will just jump into others."

"He say! You do!" barked Bonehead, stepping out of the crowd. "My dad Big Man!"

"Not of our herd," replied Mam. "We risked our lives to protect your clan, but only to repay your friends here for taking care of my son."

Bonehead looked at Stony, Echo, Hamhock, and me. *"Friends?"* he scoffed. "Me rather be friends with cats!"

Mam spoke to the crowd this time. "If this is your future Big Man, then humankind is in big trouble," she said.

Bonehead's eyes nearly popped out.

"We've been moving south for months and haven't seen a single human settlement that's survived," she continued. "A lot of bones in the snow, but that's it. No one seems to have adapted to the tigers and the cold fast enough." The throng grew around Mam as Echo interpreted her words. "I believe that the future of humankind depends on this group and the leader they choose."

A hush went through the crowd.

Mam turned to the four of us. "Woolly told us how you helped him. If you wish to join our herd, you and your families are welcome. We will protect you. But only you."

Bonehead sneered. "Go, Loony Lug! Go join herd!"

Echo gave me a look that said she was seriously considering it.

I shook my head at Boulder and Bonehead. "These are my people," I said, gesturing toward the crowd of Macrauchenia Riders and Boar Riders watching us. "I'm staying right here."

"Good," said Boulder. "Because our clan is leaving!"

I stared at him. I hadn't expected that.

"Macrauchenia Riders, follow me!" he boomed. "I know better caves! Hidden caves! Far from these nasty cats!"

The crowd stirred with excitement. Frogface and his wife, Birdbrain, immediately walked over and stood by the Big Man. They carried Bugeyes, who had recovered enough to shoot me a nasty look. Others began to follow. Then a familiar voice behind me announced: "I'm staying with Lug."

I turned around to see my father step forward. As everyone watched, my parents and sister emerged from the throng and walked over to me. "I'm proud of you," said my father, hugging me so hard I almost keeled over.

As soon as I caught my breath, I hugged him back.

"What a couple of weaklings!" jeered Boulder. "Like father, like son!"

My dad turned and looked at Boulder for a long moment. "Oh, go roll off a cliff," he said.

A few people couldn't help laughing.

Boulder's face turned about halfway between red ocher and dodo blood. Then Stony's family walked over to our side.

"Stupid traitors!" Boulder spat. He scanned the crowd menacingly. "Anyone else?"

To my amazement, Chip and Rock walked over to our side. Then their parents. Then several Boar Rider families. It wasn't long before there were many more folks around us than around Boulder. I noticed that the Big Man's forehead was starting to look as damp as a dewy leaf.

"Now, hold your stones, everyone," he wheedled, flashing a little wooden smile. "I'm just trying to protect our clans here."

"Well, then," I said, "maybe you should stay and help out?"

Boulder glared at me, but it was Bonehead who spoke.

"PEBBLEHEADS!" he screamed at the crowd. "You follow *Little Slug*?"

"His name is *Lug*," said my mother.

"Lug warned us—" said Chip.

"—about cats!" finished Rock.

"And he helped save us," Boss Hog chimed in.

"What have *you* done for us, Bonehead?" asked my sister.

Bonehead suddenly leapt at her, but Boulder grabbed his son and held him back. "Come on!" growled our ex–Big Man. "Let them be cat food!"

And with that, Boulder and his little gang stomped off into the jungle.

I thought about running up to Bonehead and grabbing the stolen club my father had made for me, but I didn't bother. I knew I'd need something much more powerful than that to stop the tigers, and I'd already gotten the best present I could ever get from my dad today.

I gazed up at the cats in the treetops. Then I looked around at all the people who had stayed with me to defend our village. I thought of Mam's words about the future of humankind depending on the leader they chose. The strange thing was that they had chosen me.

# ⊜ 19 ⊜

# A Crazy Idea

**I SAT AWAY** from everyone, my back against the Shiny Stone, gazing up at the darkening sky. I could hear the branches creaking above as the cats shifted their bodies and awaited nightfall. The snow was still coming down, but I was more concerned with the sun now. It was getting well past its peak in the sky, and dusk was not far off.

Echo walked over to me. "Hey," she said, "I never got to thank you, in the cave earlier."

"Oh," I said, "it was Mam who saved us."

"If you hadn't stepped in front of me, I'm not

sure how things would have turned out."

I looked up at the treetops. "It won't matter much if we can't scare those cats away before sunset," I said.

She leaned in and gave my cheek a kiss.

I got all tingly and jumped up—banging my head on the Shiny Stone and nearly knocking myself out.

"You okay?" she asked.

I rubbed my head and took a deep breath. "If only there was something that scared the cats like that!"

"Yeah," she said, glancing up at the sky. "Especially in the dark."

I stared at her. Her words seemed vaguely familiar. I closed my eyes and tried to remember. "Especially in the dark," I muttered. "Especially in the dark." My eyes snapped open with a sudden memory. "Of course!"

"Lug?"

But I was already darting across the clearing—no time to explain. Clambering onto Woolly's back, I whispered a few quick words in his ear. He nodded and headed for Mount Bigbigbig as fast as his legs could take us.

\\\\\\

"Strange, isn't it?" I whispered to Woolly as we stood in the snow and watched the mouth of Crag's cave flicker with light and shadow. "Last time, Echo and I thought it was a trick of the eye caused by the falling snowflakes."

Woolly eyed the entrance warily.

"Crag?" I shouted into the cave. "Crag, you in there?"

There was no answer but the howl of the wind.

I took a few cautious steps into the cave. The first thing I noticed was the warmth of the air. It felt like I'd stepped back in time—into the balmy jungle I'd known for most of my life. The farther in I ventured, the warmer the air became, and the brighter the flickering. Soon I heard the sounds of branches being broken and the strains of a scratchy voice, singing softly:

*I'll see you sooon . . .*

*When there's no mooon . . .*

*When there's a stooorm . . .*

*One must stay waaarm . . .*


Peeking around a bend into a large circular chamber, I saw Crag sitting in the center, cracking sticks with his hands. He was next to something so strange and bright that I shielded my eyes for a moment. It seemed almost alive—hot and moving, glowing orange and yellow—as if a wild little piece of the sun had escaped and been trapped by him. The hot, glowing thing seemed to emanate from several crackling pieces of wood below it. A pungent gray cloud also arose from the wood and floated out through a crack in the ceiling. Eerie flickering shadows danced on Crag's bald head and on the cave walls around him.

"Now, you be good and stay *right there*," he said, his scratchy voice full of feeling.

I was about to reply when I suddenly realized that Crag was talking to a dark gray rock he'd just put down.

He looked up as if he'd been expecting me.

"He always used to follow me around the cave," Crag explained, gently petting the rock. "But I've finally trained Cole to stay. Look how well Cole stays now."

"Um, yes . . . that's . . . impressive."

"Don't tell me, tell Cole!" Crag sighed. "He's a lonely fellow and could really use some company."

"Ah," I said, inching backward. "Good rock . . . Cole. Good rock."

Crag stroked one of his luxuriant squirrel-tail-like whiskers, his blue eyes gleaming. "So you've come for my storm light," he said, gesturing lazily toward the hot glowing thing.

I nodded. "You said it makes the beasts fear you. Especially in the dark."

He suddenly grabbed the rock again and raised it up high.

But he brought it back down again after peering at it, and I breathed a sigh of relief. "How did you get the storm light in here?" I asked.

He silently picked up a small branch and stuck the tip into the storm light. Soon the tip crackled and had its own dancing glow. My eyes must have bulged with amazement, because Crag chuckled. "You do a fair imitation of a stunned squirrel," he said, holding out the branch to me.

I stayed where I was, watching the orange-and-yellow flame slowly consume the wood. "Is it *eating* it?" I asked.

"Do squirrels eat nubnub nuts?"

"I . . . don't know."

"Me neither."

I didn't find this particularly informative, but I stepped forward and took the branch from his bony, gray-smudged hands.

"As long as you give it wood, the storm light lives," he said. "But no matter what, keep it away from water. Don't try peeing on it, believe me."

"Okay," I said, feeling the intense heat of it on my face. "Thank you."

"Don't mention it."

I gave him a grateful nod and began to back away.

"Seriously, don't mention it to anyone," he said. "Well, besides your other banished friends, of course."

"Oh," I said, "we're not banished anymore. Now there are these giant cats threatening the village, so—"

*"Not banished?"* He snatched the branch back, quick as a snake.

"Hey! What are you doing?"

"Taking what's mine," he said, tossing the branch into the storm light. "Feel free to let yourself out. And have a marvelous day!"

"What? Wait! Don't you . . . don't you want to help your own people?"

*"My* people?" He let out a soft, mirthless chuckle. *"My* people banished me."

"But you offered me the storm light when I first met you!"

"I overheard you talking to your friends that day," he said. "You said you were banished. Like me."

"I was."

Crag's bright blue eyes narrowed quizzically. "You mean . . . you're *helping* the same people who *banished* you?"

"If no one does anything, giant cats will eat them alive!"

"And that's a bad thing?"

"You know, Crag, I used to kind of envy you. I wished that I could do whatever I wanted without anyone ever bothering me. But now I see what you're like."

The man gazed silently at the storm light, his eyes narrowing.

"Look," I said, "what if I told you that all the other human clans have been wiped out by the cold?"

Crag glanced up at me. He suddenly looked very tired.

"The mammoths said they haven't seen a single human settlement that's survived," I added.

"Then," he whispered, "it's probably too late."

"Why?"

"Because the problem has gotten too big. Nothing can be done." He resumed breaking branches in the woodpile.

I cleared my throat and tried to speak calmly. "Why did they banish you?"

"Why do you care?" he snapped, cracking another branch in two.

"I thought I'd been banished because I couldn't catch a macrauchenia for the Big Game," I said. "But it was really because our Big Man didn't want me vying for power with his son."

Crag looked up. "So Boulder hasn't changed much, eh?"

I stared at him, dumbfounded.

"Now, that's more of a stunned dodo look."

"Did Boulder . . . banish you too?"

Crag shook his head. "Not exactly," he said, gazing back into the flames. "Boulder and I are about the same age. When we were kids, I was very curious about the world. I would go exploring and invent things."

"What kind of things?"

"Useful things," he said, pointing at some funny-looking objects in a dark corner, "like the feather fluffer and the rock holder."

"Never heard of them."

"Oh, I'm sure they'll be huge one day," he said. "But don't get me wrong—not all of my inventions were useful." He pointed at a strange thing with no corners lying abandoned against a wall.

"What do you call that?" I asked.

"The wheel," said Crag. "Completely useless."

I nodded.

"Anyway," he continued, "I also liked to go exploring. I was fascinated by storm light. I'd seen it strike the mountain and always wondered what happened when it did. On every stormy day, I would sneak up the mountain and look for it. One morning I got lucky and saw the storm light strike a tree. And it made *this* happen," he said, pointing to the flaming branches in front of him. "I called it *fire*."

"*Fire*," I repeated, watching it consume the stick he'd snatched back from me.

"Unfortunately, Boulder did a little sneaking of his own that day. He saw me going up the mountain and tattled to his Big Man father. They both wanted Boulder to be the next Big Man, and they somehow got the notion that I'd be his main competitor. They were wrong. I just wanted to invent and discover things. But they managed to get the council to banish me. And . . . well . . . now I talk to rocks."

I smiled.

"Glad that cheered you up," he said.

"I have some good news for you, Crag. Boulder has left the clan."

"Really?" he said. He picked up the dark gray rock he called Cole and stroked his magnificent whiskers with it. "So, Lug, if you don't catch jungle llamas and bash heads, what do you do?"

I noticed that the rock was smudging his whiskers a dark gray. "May I?"

"What?"

"Um . . . hold Cole?"

Crag suddenly looked protective. "Be gentle with him. He looks scary but he's really very sweet."

I took it. Cole didn't feel like a rock at all—it was much lighter, like dried wood. I walked over to the nearest cave wall and began using it to draw a picture of Crag.

He watched in silence.

〰〰

Crag stared at the picture of himself at his fire, while the real firelight and shadows danced over it. I glimpsed two tears travel down his cheeks and disappear into his whiskers before he turned away and looked at his woodpile. After a moment's thought, he pulled out a strong and sturdy stick the size of my arm and pushed one end of it deep into the blaze. It lit with a great crackle. "Here," he said, handing it to me. "Here is your fire."

I took it and peered at the flame. "I wish I could give you something in return."

"You already have," he said. "Now get out of here before Cole gets cranky!"

# ⊜ 20 ⊜

# LUG THE GREAT

**I CAUGHT SNATCHES** of the cats' growls as we thundered through the dark jungle, our path lit only by the flaming torch at the tip of Woolly's trunk. As the last of the sun's rays disappeared, the mammoth and I raced toward the sounds of sharp claws scrabbling down tree bark.

Once the tigers reached the ground, they were as silent as death itself. The crowd stood stock-still in the dark public clearing, listening intently.

Our torch suddenly emerged from the trees. A shout went up. The people saw how close the cats really were and ran screaming in all directions. The tigers' eyes—wide and ghostly in the darkness—blazed in the sudden light. I dismounted and took the torch from Woolly. It was about half as long now.

"So you have the storm light too?" Smilus hissed, his voice as cold as the night air. "I thought it was just that madman on the hill."

"Wrong again!" I shouted, trying to sound as dramatic as Crag. "The storm light comes from the sky, and we have tamed it to do our bidding. It will devour *anything* it touches."

Smilus eyed the flame. "And what happens when it finishes up that stick?"

I glanced around. "Woolly," I said, "hand me that branch."

The young mammoth pulled a fallen branch out of the snow and passed it to me. I thrust it into the flame. It did not light up. I tried again. Still nothing. *Stone it! It's wet,* I thought, suddenly remembering Crag's warning.

The cat grinned, his monstrous teeth gleaming a vile yellow in the firelight. "After it devours your stick, I will devour you," he said, stepping closer.

I kept the torch between us. He gave a silent nod to the tigress, and she came at me from behind.

I spun toward her. "Stay back!" I shouted.

The cats came from all sides now, forming a slowly tightening circle. I wheeled around, brandishing the torch in every direction. The ring of tigers seemed to whirl and close in around me.

The fire slowly consumed the stick, and I felt the terrible heat of it on my hand. The shorter the torch got, the more desperately I wanted to drop it. But I also knew that this flame was the only flicker of hope my clan had. I thought again of Mam's words about the future and on whom it depended. I held on even tighter.

Smilus took a step toward me. "And now," he hissed, "we're going to tear you limb from—"

"No!" said a barely visible figure emerging from the jungle. The figure dismounted from a macrauchenia. "No you won't."

I lifted up the torch to see who it was. Smilus did not wait for me, springing toward the flame with a vicious roar. I tried to move it out of his way, but he was intent on batting it, and the torch's flame accidentally brushed a line of fire across his side. He landed on top of the tigress with a yelp, the flames quickly spreading from his oily fur coat to hers. In just a few moments the entire ring of tigers was ablaze.

Shrieking, the cats hightailed it into the jungle. But this only fanned the flames. Soon we heard a dozen or so faint splashes, each followed by a shrill screech. I smiled as I recalled how cold the water was, and how the giant hairless cats must now be crawling up onto the muddy riverbank and scampering off with their bald tails between their legs.

"Lug the . . . *Great!*" shouted my dad, giving me an affectionate whack that nearly knocked me over.

The crowd cheered.

I hugged my dad again and then rushed toward the dark figure on the edge of the clearing. I raised my torch and saw Crag's wrinkly, bewhiskered face and the bundle of dry sticks he was carrying. He solemnly pulled out a stick from the bundle and touched it to my flame. There was a murmur of excitement as his torch blazed to life.

I gratefully dropped my old burnt torch in the snow and watched it go out. I turned to the crowd. "It was Crag who gave us fire!" I said.

They gazed at the thin, bewhiskered man. With Boulder and his gang gone, the faces that greeted him were mainly full of curiosity and wonder. He stared right back at some of his old childhood friends, his sprightly blue eyes twinkling in the firelight.

Crag walked to the center of the clearing. He wiped the blanket of snow off the Shiny Stone and placed his bundle of sticks on top of it. The crowd oohed and aahed as he touched his torch to the pile and a merry fire crackled to life. The Shiny Stone had never shone like this before.

"Crag the Fire Giver!" I said.

"Crag! Crag! Crag!" chanted the crowd.

\|\|\|\|\|

With both clans working together by torchlight, we quickly collected a good supply of branches. Crag showed us how to stack the wood just close enough to the flames to dry it out without burning. He also showed us how to roast bits of dodo and bananas on sticks. Soon mouthwatering aromas wafted through the air.

As we feasted around the fire, Crag told of being up on the mountaintop as a banished boy and seeing a great bolt of storm light strike a dead tree. He told of how the flames danced from branch to branch, and how he took a single burning twig back to his cave. "All of the light you see now," he said, "is descended from that single spark."

It was amazing to see Macrauchenia Riders and Boar Riders sharing a fire, and I recalled how my mother had once told me that we had all come from the same family.

My sister and I sat in the warm embrace of our parents as Mam told of the mammoths' great migration south. She told of the many wondrous sights and strange beasts. She told of the buried villages and their heedless residents, now frozen in the snow. Stories drifted through the night air like the countless brilliant embers of the fire.

Finally, when all had had their fill of food and tales, each clan went back to its village. My family insisted on going to see my art cave, and we spent the rest of the night there. My dad held up the torch, wanting to know the story behind each painting.

████

And that is how it went, at least for a while. There were beasts in the forest and biting cold, but also friendship between clans, a fire in each cave, and a story around every fire.

# ACKNOWLEDGMENTS

Bigbigbig thanks . . .

To my wonderful team at Egmont—Andrea Cascardi, Jordan Hamessley, Michelle Bayuk, Margaret Coffee, Regina Griffin, Alison Weiss, and Bonnie Cutler.

To my amazing agent, Catherine Drayton, and InkWell Management (especially Lisa Vanterpool, Masie Cochran, and Nat Jacks).

To my friends, supporters, and early readers—Al Gore, Alexis Gallagher, Angela Grossman, Anne Nesbet, Barry Wolverton, Beth Alpert, Bruce Coville, Burton Ritchie, Caroline Lawrence, Caroline Thompson, Crystal Allen, Dan Evans, Daniel Handler, David Baltimore, Deborah Halverson, Elizabeth Law, Erika Zavaleta, Gordon Korman, Greg Ferguson, Irwin Jacobs, James Campbell, Jarrett Rutland, Jay Leibold, Jen Rofe, Joe Greco, Judith Morgan, Linda Lichter, Mary Baldwin, Max Faugno, Melissa Manlove, Nathan Bransford, Patrick Carman, Peter Lerangis, Rob Taboada, Steven

Chu, Will Wister, and the Gurevich, Jain-Metzger, Nodelman, Olafsson, Rukin, Sawhney, Weiss, and Yuger families.

To fab artists Jan Gerardi, JP Coovert, and Michelle Gengaro. To my teachers and friends from CDS, Mt. Carmel, Harvard, SCBWI, Leela, and BATS Improv. To the Zeltser ladies—Asya, Aurora, Naomi, Sage, and Aunt Sarah! Most of all, to my wife, Fiona Dulbecco, and our parents—Tamara, Alex, Maureen, and Renato—for all your dedication and love.